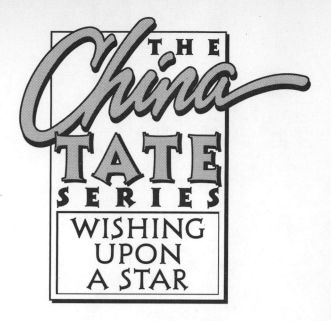

THE China TATE SERIES

WISHING UPON A STAR

LISSA HALLS JOHNSON

PUBLISHING

Colorado Springs, Colorado

D0064341

With much gratitude to
Gary and Carolyn Depolo
and
Lillian Holmlund
without whose generosity and hospitality
this book would not have been written.

WISHING UPON A STAR
Copyright © 1995 by Lissa Halls Johnson
All rights reserved. International copyright secured.
Library of Congress Cataloging-in-Publication Data
Johnson, Lissa Halls, 1955-
        Wishing upon a star/Lissa Halls Johnson.
                p.   cm. — (The China Tate series ; 4)
        Summary: As she gets to know the engaging young star of a
popular television show, China grows dissatisfied with her work at the
camp and begins to feel certain that God has sent him to Camp Crazy
Bear to help her become a celebrity herself.
        ISBN 1-56179-345-0
        [1. Camps—Fiction. 2. Christian life—Fiction. 3. Actors
and actresses—Fiction.] I. Title. II. Series: Johnson, Lissa Halls,
1955- China Tate series ; 4.
     PZ7.J63253Wi 1955
     [Fic]—dc20   94-43186
                                                              CIP
                                                              AC

Published by Focus on the Family Publishing,
Colorado Springs, Colorado 80995.
Distributed by Word Books, Dallas, Texas.

The author is represented by the literary agency of Alive
Communications, P.O. Box 49068, Colorado Springs, CO 80920.

This is a work of fiction, and any resemblance between the characters
in this book and real persons is coincidental.

Editor: Deena Davis
Cover Design: James Lebbad
Cover Illustration: Paul Casale

Printed in the United States of America
95 96 97 98 99 /10 9 8 7 6 5 4 3 2

CHAPTER ONE

CHINA TATE AND DEEDEE KIERSEY, DRESSED in shorts and sleeveless shirts, walked around the giant red cage shaped like a ball. It had steel bars and a seat in the middle of it. China looked at Kemper, shading her eyes from the piercing sun. "What's it called?"

"An atlasphere. There's all kinds of games and relays we can play with it. Today we're going to use it as a giant bowling ball."

"That's obvious," Deedee said, looking toward the five-foot foam bowling pins.

"Don't you girls ever watch *American Gladiators*?" Kemper asked.

"We don't have a TV," Deedee reminded him.

"Too bad," Kemper said, shaking his head as if an important part of their life training had been neglected.

"I doubt we're missing much," China reassured him, then mouthed to Deedee, *American Gladiators*? Grinning from ear to ear, she walked around the ball one more time. "This looks like fun. Do we get to try it?"

Kemper smiled. As usual with a new stunt, he looked

1

a little too eager and quite a bit mischievous. "Of course! Why do you think I asked you to come?"

China combed her hair back with her fingers. "Deeds, do you mind if I try first?"

"Be my guest. You can do all the trying as far as I'm concerned. Rolling around inside a ball isn't my idea of fun. Just thinking of merry-go-rounds makes my stomach urpy."

Kemper looked China over. "I don't know, you seem to have a welcome mat out for disaster. Do you think this is wise?"

"Since when did you care?" Deedee asked. "You're always getting your kids into some kind of mess . . . "

"With mud . . . " China pointed out.

"With gross things to drink . . . " Deedee added.

"And water . . . "

"And shaving cream . . . "

Kemper put up his massive hands. "Okay, okay. I give. Just remember: if anything happens, it's not my fault."

China put her hands on her hips and glared at Kemper. "Nothing is going to happen!"

She snatched the helmet from Kemper and plunked it on her head.

"Get your hair out . . . " Kemper started to say, his hands fluttering helplessly.

China took the helmet off and pulled her tawny hair back into the rubber band Deedee handed her. She replaced the helmet and tightened the chin strap. "Okay, now what?"

"I'll hold the atlasphere still," Kemper said, "while Deedee opens the hatch for you."

The giant cage looked almost like a red earthen globe. Steel bars began at the north pole, split apart, and then, at the equator, met the steel bars from the south pole. One small section hinged at the north pole and lifted up, enabling the passenger to climb in through a triangular space. China climbed in and sat on the small steel chair. Deedee let the hatch fall and latched it with a steel bolt.

"Put your feet there," Kemper said, indicating two sole-shaped pieces of steel placed against the bars. "Buckle your feet in."

China fastened the straps.

"Now put on the shoulder straps, buckling them across your body like an X."

China fumbled with the straps, adjusting them to her body. "Who rode in this thing before me? You, Kemper? These straps are adjusted for a giant."

Kemper looked sheepish. "I'm too big to fit through the hatch."

"Color me sad," China said. "Okay, now what?"

"Hold on to those handles." Kemper pointed at two steel handles straight ahead of her. "And when I say hold on to those handles, I mean hold on. Nothing, absolutely nothing, should make you let go. You hold on to those every single second or you could end up with no fingers on your hands. Understand?"

Deedee shook her head. "He sounds like my aunt. Worry, worry, worry."

"Makes you wonder how he got the job of teaching high school kids at a summer camp, doesn't it?" China asked.

"I think my dad must have felt sorry for him," Deedee said. "Or else he was desperate. Not too many people are crazy enough to take this job."

Kemper put one hand on Deedee's head and slowly pushed down until she was on her knees. "Okay, okay, I give," Deedee said, as she giggled.

China rocked her body, trying to get the 110-pound steel cage to move. "Come on, let's go! Let's get this baby rolling!"

Kemper gestured to Deedee. "Okay, girl. You get the first bowl."

"I don't weigh as much as the ball does. How do you expect me to make it work?"

"Momentum. Come on. I need to see how this will work with the kids so I'll know what rules are fair."

Deedee looked at Kemper, at the ball, then back at Kemper. "Can't you just demonstrate once for me?"

Kemper took two cushioned boat seats with straps and held them up to the red bars. "Use these to protect your hands. Once the ball gets rolling, I don't want your hands slipping between the moving bars and getting caught." He deftly pushed the ball, which rolled toward the five-foot-tall foam bowling pins. China shrieked.

Kemper ran and stopped the ball. "You okay? I didn't smash your fingers, did I? You held on, didn't you?"

China glared at him from her upside-down position. "I'm a girl, okay? I shriek when things are fun." She shook her head and turned to Deedee. "He's hopeless. I thought he knew what he was doing."

Deedee shrugged. "Like I said, Daddy felt sorry for him." In a flash, Kemper was by her side, plunging her to her knees once again. The red ball started to roll toward the driveway that led down the hill and to Grizzly Creek.

"Yoo-hoo!" China called sweetly. "Would you two please pay attention here?"

Kemper reached out and stopped the ball. "Okay, Deedee. Your turn."

Deedee took the seat cushions awkwardly in her long, slender hands. She fumbled with them and they kept falling off. "This isn't going to work. Let me just be careful. I'm not stupid, you know."

Deedee let the ball roll back toward her, then pushed forward, let it roll back once more, then gave it a huge push. Well, for her it was a huge push. The ball barely moved.

"Good roll," China said dryly.

"I'll get the hang of it," Deedee said. She pushed her mass of red curls away from her face, grabbed the steel bars, and rocked the cage ball once again. This time the ball rolled forward slightly faster than a turtle could run and knocked down one pin.

China let go of the handles. "Well, that was the ride of my life," she said, her voice as flat as old Coke. "I'm so thrilled. I'm so sick to my stomach. Please, oh please, let me out of here."

"Stop it, China," Deedee said, laughing. "I'm sorry. I'm just not strong enough."

"I am," said the voice of a stranger.

All three turned to see a high school kid, his blond hair neat but hanging loose over his right eye. A casual, friendly air clung to him. China had never seen anyone she instantly knew had his place in life all figured out. With no regrets, no questions. He just knew.

He stuck out his hand to Kemper. "Hi, I'm B.T. I'll be a camper this week. I came a little early to get my bearings. I hope that's not a problem."

Kemper shook B.T.'s hand. "No, no." He seemed a little off balance by B.T.'s calm attitude.

"I'm Deedee." Deedee stuck out her hand and smiled, looking him straight in the eyes.

"Who's the hamster?" B.T. asked, jerking his head toward the ball.

"That's China."

"Actually, I'm not a hamster, I'm a guinea pig. Mean, old Kemper has to try out all his new tortures on Deedee and me before he applies them to the campers . . . to make sure they aren't killed or harmed in any way."

In a flash, China's world began to spin around and around, over and over. She sucked in her breath so deeply that she couldn't even shriek. When the ball stopped, she was completely upside down. Kemper's dark face peered down at her. He grinned. "Girls strapped into hamster cage balls shouldn't be so eager to slam big men who can give them whirlwind spins, should they?"

China shook her head, which felt like it would burst at any moment. "No, Mr. Kemper," she said solemnly. "I will never do that again."

Kemper set her upright, then smacked his hands together. When he turned away, China stuck her tongue out at him and waggled her fingers from her ears. When B.T. and Deedee started to laugh, Kemper spun around. But China sat serenely, her hands gripping the red handles.

"Do I get to try?" B.T. asked. "Bowling is an occasional hobby of mine."

Kemper stood back. "Be my guest. Maybe you should use these seat cushions to protect your hands."

"Nah. I'll probably do better if I can get a good grip." B.T. grabbed the bars below the equator and pulled up. His muscles bulged, giving proof he probably worked out. His hands moved slowly, firmly, and with great strength. The ball moved forward at a rapid clip, scattering the bowling pins.

"STRIKE!" everyone yelled together, high fives resounding.

B.T. grabbed the ball and pulled it backward toward the starting line. He stopped to say something to Kemper just as Deedee started to scream. "It's on my foot! It's on my foot! Quick! Move it off!"

B.T. gave the giant cage a shove and quickly bent down to check Deedee's foot. Kemper knelt with him. Deedee dropped to the ground and let B.T. loosen the laces on her hiking boot.

China watched them slowly turn upside down, move through the blur of trees, then land right side up again. "This is trippy," she breathed softly to herself. China imagined there was no gravity or that the earth had suddenly switched places with the sky. She liked watching everything move about so dreamily. But then it seemed to be moving faster. Earth, sky. Earth, sky. The cage rumbled. then picked up speed. "Guys!" she called, trying to sound calm. "Uh, guys? Yoo-hoo! B.T.? Kemper?" As she felt herself really start to roll, she let out a new shriek. "KEMPER!"

China hoped they looked up to see her giant red hamster ball rolling toward the stream. *Hold on,* she reminded herself. *Don't let go of the handles. No matter what happens, don't let go!*

Words popped out of her mouth from the frightened place inside. "I'm gonna die! I'm a-gonna DIE!"

The cage, rolling over rocks and pebbles, threw them

inside at China, pelting her bare legs and arms. She clamped her eyes shut to keep the stinging dirt from doing more damage. The cage rattled and bounced. China's teeth rattled and chomped. For once she was glad she had short nails. Otherwise her white-knuckled grip on the handles would have driven them deep into her flesh. Hollow thuds whacked her helmet as her head banged the bars.

"China!" Kemper's voice bellowed. "Hold on, we're coming!"

China could hear nothing but Kemper's voice over the racket of the bouncing, rattling cage. She tried to picture how far it was to the creek. And what was beyond if the creek didn't stop her.

That stupid B.T.! If I live through this, I'm going to kill him! The more China thought about B.T., the angrier she got. With every smacking stone, with every bang of her head, China added a new grudge to her list. *I'm going to get him! I'm going to get him good, even if it's the last thing I ever do.*

CHAPTER TWO

Just when China thought the rattling cage would blow apart, she felt a cold spray of water. The atlasphere rolled through Grizzly Creek, thoroughly dunked her head, paused at the opposite bank, then rolled backward before coming to a stop in the middle of the deepest, coldest, fastest part of the creek.

China clutched the handles, not sure what else to do. The ball had stopped on the equator so that China faced the water, her back arched in the air. All her weight pushed against the body straps that held her in. The frigid water rushed beneath her belly, pummeling her arms and legs. China let go of the handles and moved her hands out of the water to grasp the bars around the north pole. She stared at the water rushing beneath her stomach, wondering what to do next. The entry/escape hatch was to her right. If she set the shoulder/waist straps free, she would fall face first into the water. And unless she could undo the foot straps, she would be worse off.

Reaching into the water, she fumbled for the foot

straps. But the force of the water was too strong, and she couldn't loosen them. She thought about rocking the cage, but if it rolled the wrong way, her head would be in the water and she'd drown. She decided it would be best to wait and hang there.

Soaked to the skin, China shivered. The warm air suddenly felt freezing. She hoped the water wouldn't push her to a different position. The pounding water stole any sounds of rescue from her ears, and she certainly couldn't see anything from her position. So she set her mind on a plot to get back at B.T.

Trying to roll him down the same rocky path would be perfect . . . but that was too obvious for revenge. I could . . . well, what could I do to a camper? I be sent home in a split second if I tried to do something. Her thoughts weren't terribly consistent. They kept getting interrupted by her fear that the ball would roll again. Water sprayed her face as if she were an obnoxious new obstacle to its current. She'd never thought before how relentless water could be. *Where does it come from? How can it keep on coming and coming and coming?*

At last, she heard different sloshing sounds. "China!" Deedee screamed at her over the charging water. "Are you okay?"

China tried to nod her head and shake it at the same time. Her neck muscles had grown sore and stiff.

Three sets of legs sloshed through the water and surrounded her cage. Silence. Then laughter in unison.

Kemper's deep, "Heh, heh, heh," Deedee's foghorn sucking in air, and B.T.'s delightful laugh, full of air and joy.

China turned her head toward the unfamiliar laugh. B.T.'s hands grasped the cage, his face lit with happy surprise. And something else. Even though China didn't know him, his look was an unmistakable, "Did I do that?" And yet there was laughter dancing at the corners of his eyes. Did he know what would happen before he shoved her? Did he do it on purpose? Or did he laugh because, let's face it, it really was pretty funny? China could picture herself from a distance, hanging there, her feet dangling in the water.

But China didn't want to see it that way. She wanted to stay mad. And it didn't help that everybody stood there laughing at her.

"Okay, the ride's over. The show has ended. Get me out of here!" China demanded.

The three spectators looked at each other, then at the ball in the middle of the creek.

B.T. started chattering. "We could roll her out of here real quickly, but then her head would go under the water again and we could get it stuck on a rock. But if we unclasp her wrong, she'll get hurt, and she could be hurt already, or, on the other hand . . . "

"SHUT UP!" China screamed. "You think I want anyone to listen to you? You are a complete idiot! Someone else just DO something!" China demanded, trying her best to give them her angriest look from this difficult position.

She knew she didn't fool Deedee for one instant. Kemper, on the other hand, seemed to come to life. "I'll hold the ball steady. B.T., you open the hatch and hold it open. Deedee, you help China come out of the restraints."

Everyone moved at once.

"This whole thing is so furfuraceous!" B.T. shouted over the roar of the water.

Deedee stared at him. "Excuse me?"

"I said this whole thing is furfuraceous."

"What's that supposed to mean?"

"You guys!" China shouted. "Forget what the stupid word means. Just get me out of here NOW."

Kemper braced his body against the ball on the downstream side of the creek.

"It means 'covered with dandruff,'" B.T. said.

Deedee unfastened one strap, then turned to stare at him. "That doesn't even make sense."

"It's not supposed to," B.T. admitted.

"Get me down, Deedee!"

Deedee spun around and unfastened China's feet. Then she carefully undid the shoulder/waist straps while China held on to the rungs over her head. China swung down, stood in the water, and stepped through the hatch. Glaring at B.T., she said, "*You* are a jerk."

China tried to navigate the creek, but her equilibrium

was off from the hair-raising trip down the hill and hanging at an odd angle until she was rescued. She took two steps forward, slipped, and fell.

B.T. reached out and caught her in his arms. "Well, if this isn't totally hackbut, I don't know what is."

China scowled at him. "Let go of me!"

"No. You'll fall again."

"Let go of me!"

B.T. dramatically opened his arms and backed up. China again lost her balance and fell.

"See?" B.T. said calmly. "You hate to admit it, but you need me."

"I don't need you," China stated sarcastically. "I only need your arms to help me get to the side of the creek."

B.T. peered through his hair and said, "As you wish."

China thought she'd die right then. Or melt. Or fall apart. But she'd never admit it to this arrogant B.T. Never in a million years. China hated the fact that B.T. couldn't help being adorable. He just was. Looking out through that thatch of blond hair that hung over one piercing blue eye, he could kill her with a look. No matter how mad she was at the guy, she couldn't stay mad for long. She could pretend, but she couldn't quite stay there. *Besides,* she thought, *adorable guys never pay attention to me. They are so stuck on their looks, they don't have time for anyone but the Heathers of this world.*

Kemper huffed and puffed and sweated a thousand

drops of sweat before he managed to roll the heavy ball through the opposing water.

Deedee dropped on to the rocks next to China at the side of the creek. She shaded her eyes as she looked up at B.T. "So what's the deal with the weird words?"

B.T. stood with his legs spread far apart and crossed his muscular arms. If he'd been bald and wore an earring, he would have looked like the genie guy on the Mr. Clean bottle. He shrugged. "I like words that sound funny. It doesn't really matter if they mean anything even closely related to what I use them for."

"Like furfu . . . whatever you said."

"Furfuraceous."

"Yeah. The atlasphere escape isn't really like dandruff."

"No, it just sounded like it fit."

China took off her helmet. Water had caught inside and now ran down her body in cold rivulets. She stared at this strange yet positively adorable person. She wanted desperately to hate him. But there was something so irresistibly lovable about him that she'd rather pull him next to her and cuddle him for the rest of her life. *There's no way I'm going to give him the satisfaction of thinking I'm not mad*, she thought, *because I am.*

B.T. went on. "There's lots of really funny-sounding words that mean something kind of bad. So I don't use those. I only use ones that have totally innocuous meanings."

"Like hackbut?" China snapped. "If that one doesn't mean something bad, I'll eat my shoe."

"It means a gun barrel." He paused, his compelling blue eyes growing dark with concern. "That's not bad, is it?"

"Only if you're pointing it at someone," China replied.

Deedee leaned over and started to untie China's shoe.

China slapped at her hand. "What are you doing?"

Deedee's eyes danced. "I can't wait to see you eat this thing."

"Good idea!" B.T. said, bending down to help.

"You guys!" shrieked China. "Lay off!"

Deedee nimbly undid the wet shoelace, and B.T. snatched her shoe off. He held it up to her face. "Come, now, China dear. Time for a snack."

"NO!" China laughed. "Get away!"

China fell backward. Deedee pounced on her, pinching her nose so she'd have to open her mouth. China squirmed beneath her friend, trying to shake her off. B.T. managed to get the toe of the shoe in China's mouth.

"Hey, B.T.!" Kemper's voice boomed.

B.T. dropped the shoe and jumped to his feet. "Yeah?"

"I could use your help rolling this thing back up the hill."

"Sure thing!"

Deedee got off China and helped her up. She looked at the two guys struggling to push the giant ball up the hill. "B.T. is incredibly gorgeous."

China shoved her foot into her ratty tennis shoe and shrugged. "I guess, if you like jerks."

"China!" Deedee scrutinized her friend's face.

China focused on tying her shoe.

"He's not a jerk," Deedee insisted.

China thought a moment, trying desperately to put his smile, his eyes, his whole self, out of her mind. "He is, at the very least, incredibly stupid."

"Why would you say that?"

"Oh, come on, Deedee! He rolls the ball right on top of your foot . . . "

"An honest mistake."

"And then he corrects it by shoving me down the blasted hill!"

Deedee smiled softly. She looked across the creek and shook back her hair. "I thought it was sweet that he was so concerned about my foot that he didn't even think about anything but helping me."

China's mouth dropped open. "I can't believe it, Deedee Kiersey! I think you're in love!"

Deedee turned to look China full in the face. "It's him, you know."

"Him who?"

"The guy friend you've been looking for."

"Is not!" China shouted, turning red.

"Is too," Deedee said softly.

"Why would you think an insane thing like that?"

Deedee shrugged, then twirled a curl around her finger. "Feminine intuition." She smiled. "He thinks you're cute, you know."

"Does not."

"Does too."

"Does not." China jumped up and stomped toward the lake. Away from the hill. Toward home. How could Deedee think she could ever possibly like this idiot? Or that he could possibly like her even as a friend?

China emerged from the bedroom in dry clothes. Deedee sat on the sofa, cuddling her little sister Anna. "I invited B.T. to go horseback riding with us after lunch" she said.

"Then I'm not going."

"Oh, China! Don't be a jerk!"

"Now I'm the jerk?"

"Give the guy another chance."

Anna popped her thumb out of her mouth. "Jerk," she said plainly, then popped her thumb back in.

Both girls stared at her. "What did you say, Anna?" Deedee gently pulled Anna's thumb out. But Anna just looked at her big sister and smiled.

China went over and kissed Anna on the top of her bandaged head. "I'm glad you're talking again, sweetie." Anna had been injured the week before, and the doctor had warned them she might not speak again for a long time.

"Even if her first word is not one we should tell Mom about," Deedee added.

China ate lunch, lost deep in thought. She wanted to hate B.T. She wanted to be mad at him. But Deedee was probably right. He really didn't mean to do anything bad to anyone. And she probably had looked awfully funny hanging there in that stupid ball.

CHAPTER THREE

B.T. LEANED AGAINST A HITCHING POST, waiting for the girls. On top of his head sat a genuine black cowboy hat. His cowboy shirt swirled purples and blues with pearlescent buttons. Black jeans and multicolored leather cowboy boots completed his ensemble. As the girls approached, he unfolded his arms from across his chest and tipped his hat to each one in turn. "ma'am," he said in a thick cowboy twang, indicating China. "ma'am," he said to Deedee.

China willed her heart to stop beating wildly. *This is stupid! He's only an idiot trying to impress us. I refuse to be impressed. I refuse to be impressed. I refuse . . .*

B.T. moseyed over to a large buckskin mare, and in one smooth move, he popped a strand of hay between his teeth, crossed his arms, dropped his right foot, toe down in front of the left, and let his body lean into the rump of the horse.

Deedee opened her mouth to say something, then seemed to think better of it, running her fingers through her thick mop of curls instead. She let the

20

beginnings of a smile touch the edges of her mouth. She discreetly put out her hand low, signaling China to stand still. The girls waited. But not for long.

The mare turned and stared at the rude intruder who would consider her queenly body a lamppost. She stepped her hind legs away from B.T. He couldn't unfold himself quickly enough to stand gracefully as he stumbled and swung around to face the horse. "What do you think you're doing, you gutbucket?"

The mare flipped open her lips and bared her teeth at him, tossing her head as if she hoped she really weren't tied to the post.

"Oh, be that way," B.T. muttered. He composed himself and turned to the girls, speaking again in his best cowboy twang, which actually was excellent. "Ladies, a real man would never allow a lady to be thrust into incredible danger by being forced to ride such an unruly beast. Please allow me."

Deedee smiled and gestured. "We accept your kindness." Out of the side of her mouth, Deedee told China, "This ought to be great."

Deedee showed China and B.T. where the saddles were, and each took the one designated for their horse. The ranch hand waved at Deedee. "You sure you don't want me to go with you?"

B.T. answered, "No, sir. I'll be responsible for these ladies."

The ranch hand rolled his eyes and waved them away.

Every time B.T. moved, he hooked his thumbs into his belt loops and sauntered as though he'd been a cowboy his whole life. She knew better, because he could certainly act like a cowboy, but he obviously didn't know the first thing about horses. China didn't know a lot about them either, but she knew enough not to walk around a horse's backside without letting it know you were there. He also threw the saddle blanket on the middle of the horse's back rather than up close to her neck on the withers. Every time he made some mistake, his horse would stop munching and open her lips to show him her teeth.

Deedee walked over to B.T. and turned on her usual hospitable charm. In a quiet voice, not the least bit condescending, she instructed him on the finer points of saddling a horse. Then she left him to complete her own saddling task.

"Okay, girl," he said, slapping the horse's rump, "you're ready for a day's work rounding up strays and driving those cattle home!" The buckskin gave him the usual look, only without the teeth, and nodded her head.

"Hey, look!" B.T. said in his normal voice. "She agrees with me."

"Did you tighten the cinch?" Deedee asked.

"Of course I tightened the cinch," B.T. replied. He unwrapped the reins from the hitching post and led the horse to the center of the corral.

B.T. stomped his feet and moved his hands on his thighs as if trying to get his jeans to move down over his boots. "What's her name, anyway?" he asked. "You should always call a lady by her name."

"Sadie," Deedee replied.

"Sadie, m'lady," B.T. said, stroking her velvet nose. Sadie jerked her head up, almost ripping the reins from B.T.'s hands.

"Sadie doesn't like anyone to touch her face," Deedee told him.

"Seems Sadie doesn't like a lot of things," B.T. said. He led her over to the watering trough, but Sadie didn't seem interested.

B.T. stomped his feet again, but that didn't seem to shift the uncomfortable jeans. So he finally bent over at the waist to tug at the pants hem. At that moment, Sadie decided to get her revenge. She tucked her head down, made contact with the seat of B.T.'s pants, and gave a good nudge. Water sprayed everywhere as B.T. landed face first in the water trough. Sadie nodded her head and whinnied softly.

China and Deedee burst out laughing. B.T. slowly rolled over and sat in the mucky water. He grabbed his hat, scooped up a hatful of water, and plunged it over his head. Water poured down his body, sending the girls into new laughter. B.T. played it like a pro—every movement like that of an actor milking the moment for laughs. And he got plenty of them. When he finally stepped out of the trough, he put his hands on his hips and stared Sadie square in her brown eyes. "Well, girl, I guess we're even now."

B.T. looked at the girls. "Anything crazy that happens around me seems to happen on its own. Like the hamster cage this morning. You probably thought I did it on purpose."

China stared at him, determined not to acknowledge that her feelings for him might be changing. She didn't want him to know he was disarming her at every turn.

"I'm a magnet for this kind of stuff. One thing to remember. I'm never serious. Everything's fun. There's no time to be serious in this worn-out world." B.T. slapped his hands together. "Well! That's as serious as I'll ever get." He picked up Sadie's reins. "Come on, Sadie, m'lady. We've got some riding to do."

China and Deedee swung on to their mounts and waited for B.T. As he put his right foot into the right stirrup, Deedee said "NO!" so sharply that B.T. quickly backed up.

"What?"

"Never mount a horse on the right side. Especially Sadie. She'll nip your butt if you do."

B.T. smiled and said under his breath, "I knew that." He walked around to the other side of the horse and put his left foot in the stirrup. Sadie was up so high and B.T.'s leg was so bent that he had trouble getting the leverage to pop himself into the saddle. As he stood there in that awkward position, he held the reins too tight. Sadie started walking in a circle, and B.T. hopped around backward. "Sadie, luv, do me a favor. Hold still." Sadie ignored him. She seemed to be rather enjoying this awkward dance.

Deedee and China broke into such fits of laughter they could hardly speak. Deedee finally managed, "Let loose on the reins."

B.T. dropped the reins altogether, and Sadie thought this a grand time to bolt toward freedom. B.T. plopped to the dirt, which instantly turned to mud on his wet pants.

China tried hard not to laugh, but tears came to her eyes. She could keep silent for only so long, then a loud hiccup broke her vow of silence.

"Do you want the ranch hand to help?" Deedee offered.

"No, thanks," B.T. said as he trotted after Sadie. There wasn't any place for her to run, so he was able to corner her. Using the fence rail, he hoisted himself up on his mighty steed.

Deedee took up the lead, China fell in behind her, and B.T. took the rear. They hadn't gone fifty yards when China thought she heard an odd noise. A kind of huffing and grunting. She turned to peer over her shoulder and saw B.T. riding almost sideways, his saddle slowly slipping down Sadie's side.

"Uh," B.T. said, "I think I'm having a slight problem."

"Nothing a moment of rest won't cure," he said with a comical British accent.

"Deeds," China called out, "our knight in dull armor is having difficulty with his steed."

Deedee wheeled her black gelding, Midnight, around and trotted back over the rough terrain. She looked at B.T. and his predicament and said calmly, "I don't think you tightened the cinch enough."

Deedee tree-tied Midnight and dismounted to help B.T. off his horse. She then replaced the saddle and tightened the cinch. When it seemed tight enough, B.T. said, "Oh, that's better!"

"No, it isn't," Deedee said. She punched Sadie in the gut, and when Sadie exhaled, Deedee quickly pulled the cinch up tighter.

"Ow! Isn't that mean?"

"'Course not. Sadie's a pro at blowing out her stomach. She delights in dropping riders."

B.T. used a boulder to pop back on Sadie, and the trio resumed their ride.

For the next hour, they acted completely silly. B.T. moved in and out of voices and characters so fast that the girls could only laugh in response.

China looked over her shoulder. "You know, B.T., you ought to be an actor or something."

B.T. looked at her oddly. Not like he considered what she had said, but like what she had said was funny. A huge smile took over his whole face, lighting his eyes with a brightness China hadn't seen before. "Why, thank you, ma'am. That comes as quite a compliment."

The trail widened and the horses traveled side by side, their hooves clacking against the rocks. "So why are you guys so privileged?" B.T. asked.

"Privileged?"

"Yeah. How come you get the horses, the first atlasphere ride?"

Deedee clucked her horse to step up the pace a little. "My dad is the director of the whole campground."

"Mr. Kiersey?"

"You know him?"

B.T. adjusted his hat. "I talked with him some." He yanked his foot backward, as Sadie kept turning her head as though to bite him. "This horse sure is a pain."

"She's old and temperamental," Deedee told him.

"Like my grandmother," B.T. offered. The girls laughed.

"The ranch hand keeps telling me she's not going to make it another summer."

"I hope not," B.T. said, moving his foot out of the way again. "What about you, China? Your dad the head of something else?"

"My dad's in Guatemala. I'm just along for the ride."

"Explain, please."

"I'm an MK from Guatemala."

"What's an MK?"

"Missionary Kid. My parents are missionaries there.

I was supposed to come to the States to spend the summer with my aunt Liddy and ended up here instead. I'm working in the kitchen."

"Have you guys always been friends?"

"It seems like it," Deedee said, smiling at China.

"Time for a theological discussion," Deedee announced.

"Can you deal with this, B.T.?" China asked.

B.T. shrugged. "I suppose. I might learn something."

"Too bad," China teased. "I had hoped you'd be miserable."

"Thank you. You are too kind."

"You're welcome." China smiled at Deedee. "If you think you must drag us into your tortured mind, go ahead."

"Okay," Deedee said cheerfully. "Do you really think God has a reason for everything?"

"Every tiny thing?" asked China.

"Yeah. Every detail of your life."

"No."

"Not anything?"

"Some things. But not all."

"Like what?" Deedee's brows had drawn together, so China knew she was dead serious.

"Like I don't think God has a reason for me meeting B.T." China smiled a fake smile at B.T.

B.T. smiled back. "Why, thank you again!"

"God had a reason for you and Heather to be here together."

"Who's Heather?" B.T. asked.

China rolled her eyes and ignored him. "I don't think so. Not unless God is in the torture business."

"Heather was China's fave friend in the whole world," Deedee teased.

China wished she could throw a dirt clod. A blood clot. Anything.

Deedee continued. "Don't you think God had a reason for you going to Aunt Liddy's?"

"The only reason God had for that was to get me here."

"Can I say something here?" B.T. interjected. "I know God has me here, at this camp, this week, for some reason."

"You really believe that?" Deedee asked, not unkindly.

"You bet! I've seen God do some wild things that seemed to have no purpose. But it always ends up like the puzzle of my life would be missing a piece without it."

"Why does God want you here?" China asked. "To torture me? Kill me?"

B.T. winked. "Could be."

Deedee sat up straighter in her saddle. "All these speakers come and talk about how God brought all these people together for a reason. And I can't help but wonder if someone out there wasn't listening to God and came anyway. Like they barged through a door that wasn't meant for them."

"Can you do that?" China asked. "What if God needs my help—he points to the door and I have to go find a way to open it?"

B.T. shook his head. "I think if God wants you to go through a door, he'll open it and you won't have to force anything."

"I don't know," China said, shaking her head. "He's going to have to do something pretty drastic to get me to change this one."

B.T. held up his hands, "Whoops! I wouldn't challenge God like that if I were you."

"I'm not challenging God," China protested.

Deedee butted in. "Now for the million-dollar question."

China rolled her eyes. "Can't take a little conflict, huh?"

Deedee ignored her. "If you had a million dollars, what would you do with it?"

China looked at B.T. "Like that's really going to happen."

B.T. turned away, and looked up the mountainside.

"Come on, China. What would you do with a million dollars?" Deedee persisted.

"I'd buy a camp like this and pay for all the poor kids to come and enjoy one week at camp."

B.T. turned to look at her, his blue eyes seeming to search her out. He nodded almost imperceptibly.

"Your turn, Deedee," China said.

"What about B.T.?"

"No, you go ahead," B.T. said. "Ladies always first." He grinned at her with a killer smile. Deedee returned it. *Shoot!* China thought. *They'd be a dynamite pair. Two smiles that could wipe you off the mountain.*

Dust billowed beneath the horses' hooves. Midnight snorted.

"I think I would probably travel," Deedee said. B.T. and China watched her. "I don't know. Go somewhere very different and exciting. Madagascar. Kenya. Greece."

"But you have to sunbathe topless in Greece," China reminded her.

"Forget Greece. Or I'll stay away from the beaches."

"Would you take a friend?" China asked teasing.

"Of course," Deedee said right away. "But, hmm. . . I don't know who that would be."

China whacked her with the reins. Deedee kicked Midnight and they were off in a cloud of dust. China spurred her horse, Sundance, who went off at a half-hearted trot. Sadie picked up her head and trotted after them, B.T.'s legs bouncing every which way, his body jostling around in the saddle. He clutched the saddle horn with both hands. "Can you get this horse to stop?" he asked, his voice as jumpy as his body.

"No, but you can," China called back over the clattering hooves. "Pull back on the reins firmly and tell her 'Whoa.'"

B.T. yanked on the reins. Sadie came up off her front

feet in a half hearted rear, landed hard, and then snorted and shook her head. B.T. went white.

China stifled a laugh.

B.T. glared at her. "You said to pull back on the reins."

"Yeah. Firmly. I didn't say to yank."

Deedee, Midnight, and their cloud of dust returned. "That was no fun. You're supposed to chase me."

"B.T. had a slight problem."

B.T. fanned himself with his hat. "Nothin' a cowboy cain't handle, ma'am."

China smirked and turned Sundance around. "Let's go."

"Hey, B.T.," Deedee said, "you didn't answer the million-dollar question."

"Maybe he doesn't want to," China said.

"A cowboy don't say nuthin' he don't want to," B.T. agreed.

"Too bad," Deedee said. "This isn't an optional question. When you go riding with me, you have to be ready to spill your guts."

"I almost spilled them on the rocks," B.T. muttered.

"So? What would you do if you had a million dollars?"

B.T. stared up into the mountains again. China, riding next to him, could see his jaw clench and unclench. When he turned to face them again, his eyes had a deep serious look to them. "I'd give it away—in exchange for a true friend." He turned back to consider the mountain.

Then, without any kind of warning, B.T. vanished. Well, not like in thin air. But Deedee and China were riding along watching him, trying to figure him out, when suddenly, almost like a cartoon, he was there and then he was on the ground. His hat hung in the air a moment longer than he did, then it too dropped to the ground.

Both girls reined in their horses and jumped down. B.T. sat, looking quite bewildered. Sadie lay there as crumpled as a horse can get. "What did you do to the poor horse?" Deedee cried.

"What did your poor horse do to me?" B.T. countered. He stood up, rubbing his backside, and gently shoved his boot into the horse. "Come on, Sadie. It can't be that bad."

Deedee stuck her ear down to the horse, seemed to smell her nose, and in general looked like a paramedic at work.

China put her hand on B.T.'s arm. "Are you okay?"

"I think my pride is wounded, ma'am. Nuthin' else."

China looked at his backside. "I never heard it called a pride before."

B.T.'s bewildered look metamorphosed into a smile of approval.

"Sadie's dead," Deedee said, amazed.

B.T. took off his hat and scratched his head. "Do you try to give it CPR or something?"

Deedee stared at the horse. "When the ranch hand

said she might drop dead someday, I didn't think he meant it literally."

"Now what?" B.T. asked. "Zareba fungoid. We can't drag her back."

"You'll have to ride with one of us," Deedee said authoritatively. "Or rather, one of us will have to ride with you."

"Sadie's not going far, Miss," B.T. said in his drawl.

Deedee shook her head, laughing. "What I meant was, you'll have to sit in the saddle, and one of us will have to ride behind."

Deedee looked at Midnight and then at Sundance. Her mental wheels spun so loud, China could almost hear them. "Sundance is the bigger, quieter horse. Midnight is a little too frisky. Better put the two of you on Sundance."

China felt her stomach flip. She threw Deedee a look. Deedee just smiled back as if she hadn't caught China's meaning.

"Well, little filly," B.T. said to China after mounting Sundance, "we'll make sure you arrive back to the ranch safely." He put out his hand to help China up. China slipped her foot into Deedee's linked hands as a makeshift stirrup. She clasped B.T.'s hand and swung herself on to the horse's back.

The simple activity made China's head spin. She felt totally stupid. Her insides were all jumbled together. "Zareba fungoid," she muttered. He smelled of sweat.

And new clothes with the tags just torn off. And horse. And something else. Drakkar Noir? Maybe. Something richer.

B.T. laughed. "Here. Put your arms around my waist. I won't bite."

B.T. seemed so calm about the whole thing. As if he had girls riding on the back of his horse every day. Like it was no big deal.

And in lots of ways it wasn't. He was just another guy. Just another person on the earth. But it didn't feel that way inside. She wanted to hate him. Instead, she felt like she'd found something she'd lost long ago and didn't even know it was lost until right this minute. She felt connected somehow. She'd had boyfriends before. But that wasn't what this felt like. It felt comfortable. Like something that was meant to be. A friend like Deedee. Only male. The friend she'd always wanted. It was something she couldn't put her finger on. But it was there, as solid as the horse underneath her.

But a guy like him would never give a girl like me a second thought. Not in a million years. Not for a million dollars. Especially since I've been so mad at him, she thought.

China's heart felt sad because she'd finally found something that seemed so right. And it was out of reach.

Beneath her hands, she felt B.T. sigh. And a peace came rumbling through.

CHAPTER FOUR

THE RANCH HAND DIDN'T SEEM PARTICULARLY surprised about Sadie. "Yep, she was an old one."

"What'll you do about her?" Deedee asked.

"Take the truck up. Get the saddle. Then have the glue company come get her."

Deedee made a face. "Sorry I asked."

China nudged Deedee. "It's almost four o'clock."

"Thanks for letting us ride," Deedee said to the ranch hand. "Come on, I gotta get out of here."

"What's the hurry?" B.T. asked, his long, smooth strides easily keeping up with Deedee's long-legged steps.

"I'm supposed to give out cabin assignments to the new campers coming in."

"Like me?"

Deedee looked at him with her head tilted. "I keep forgetting you're supposed to be a camper. Somehow you don't fit."

"Never have, never will," he said with a wry smile.

The trio walked past Little Bear Lake and up to the

kiosk near Eelapuash, the dining hall. The whole way there, campers seemed to look at them, then suddenly stare. Mouths dropped open. A flurry of whispers showered around them. Girls giggled and put a shield of hands over their mouths so the trio couldn't see what was being said. Guys were more cool about it. They did a kind of double take and then would nod at the group. China shot Deedee a questioning look; Deedee answered with a shrug of her shoulders. Both looked at B.T., who seemed oblivious to the whole thing.

"Will you give me a tour of the camp, China?" B.T. asked.

"I don't know it as well as Deedee."

"But Deedee has to work. I'll take whatever you know. I just don't want to get lost."

China nodded without much emphasis. The kids around her were too distracting. All her anger had melted away. But she still didn't want to let down her guard. Didn't want to get hurt believing one of her wildest dreams could come true.

Deedee disappeared inside the kiosk, then reappeared when she opened the shuttered wooden window. Immediately an irregular line of kids snaked away from the wooden hut. Deedee whipped a clipboard from an unseen shelf and flipped open the pages to the boys' cabin assignments. "B.T., I don't know your last name."

B.T. pulled his cowboy hat lower over his eyes. "A cowboy don't give his name to just anybody, ma'am." Then he leaned forward and said quietly, "I'll get my assignment later." He grabbed China's hand and slipped away from the crowd.

Instantly, China was in another time zone where this wasn't happening. It couldn't be. This was only a fluke.

As soon as they were on their way, B.T. dropped her hand. "Sorry about that," he said. "I really shouldn't have grabbed your hand like that. But I wanted to get out of there."

"That's okay," China said hesitantly, not sure what to think. "My aunt hates crowds," she offered, trying to make him feel better. *See? That's all it was—a way to escape.*

B.T. started to do a little skipping step. A lighthearted jumping thing. "I'm so excited to be at camp. I've never been, you know."

"You're going to love it."

"Okay. Give me the rundown. What can I expect? Who am I? Where am I going? What is the meaning of life?"

"You can expect Kemper to make your life miserable with gross, disgusting games."

"The atlasphere wasn't disgusting."

"No, just dangerous."

Doffing his hat, B.T. spun around and around, his head tilted back, his arms out. Then he stopped cold.

"Don't tell anyone you saw me do that."

China tilted her head. "Why should anyone care?"

"It's not terribly cool, you know. Us dudes are supposed to be cool all the time. Walk cool. Talk cool. Use our hands in these low, small gestures. Nothing outrageous. Nothing to draw attention. Cool is supposed to draw attention."

China laughed. "Ahh! So that's the secret! I just thought guys had no life. No nutty bone in their bodies."

"Oh, they're there, all right. But we can't ever show them. Can't ever be nuthin' but cool." He started to strut in an ultra-cool, ultra-smooth glide with just enough body movement to almost be jerky. "I'm cool, baby. I don't have emotions. Unless we're talking righteous anger here. Nope. I don't cry. I don't get excited. I'm just cool. Nothing fazes me."

China couldn't stand it anymore. She thought her insides were going to bust right out into the open.

B.T. jumped in China's way, blocking her path, his macho stance a perfect mimic of a mafioso boss. "So tell me, girlie-girl. How is it that girls can be so, so, uh . . . "

"Dramatic?"

"Yeah, that's the word, girlie-girl. Dramatic. Man, you girls can cry in front of everyone. Stomp that foot. Shriek. Be so expressive with your eyes, yet pretend we can't read them. How? Why?"

China stared at the dirt, digging into it with her toe. "We aren't that bad, are we?"

"I suppose not. At least you tone it down when guys come around. I see it from a distance, but the minute I get close, whammo! The walls go up and this body language comes on. Does a girl think about anything other than getting a guy to like her?"

China looked up, startled.

B.T. caught himself and waved his hat. "Sorry, sorry. Trade secrets, I know."

She swallowed hard. "Do you think I'm only trying to get you to like me?" she asked in horror.

B.T. smiled, his hair falling over that one blue eye. "If I did, I wouldn't be here."

He spun around and walked away, his arms limp and swinging at his sides. His legs became rubbery. She ran to catch up with him. "You're such an ape."

His lips pooched out and flapped. "Oooh! Oooh! Ahh! Ahh!"

"Here, let's go to Eelapuash and I'll introduce you to Magda."

"Eelapuash?"

"Means 'sore belly' in some Native American tongue."

B.T. nodded his approval, giving her a thumbs-up. "It's about time someone labeled cafeteria food what it really is."

China led him around the back of the building and

pushed open the screen door. "Magda?" she called. "I have someone here to meet you."

Magda rounded the corner, wiping her hands on her apron, her face welcoming whoever would be there. In the briefest of moments, China saw B.T.'s face relax just the tiniest bit. And some unseen ray of connection whammed from Magda to B.T. and back again. B.T.'s arms flew open and he rushed at her. They acted like they knew each other from somewhere before.

"Magda!" he cried as he hugged her tight. "I swear you are my Granny Whipple's twin."

Magda beamed and held him as China imagined she held her own son. When they separated, Magda brushed the lock of hair away from his eyes. "You really ought to cut that so we can see your beautiful blue eyes," she scolded.

B.T. hung his head in mock shame. "I know, Maggie."

China cringed and closed her eyes, waiting for the blast of correction from Magda. She slowly opened her eyes, prepared to see wisps of steam curling up into the air. Instead of steam, rays of sunshine beamed from Magda to her new boy.

China wondered what in the world was going on here. B.T. seemed to have something China had always wanted—the ability to see inside people and immediately know what kind of person they were. He had such ease around new people. Such a way to make them feel at ease . . . make them feel special.

"B.T.," China said, "come meet Rick."

Magda shook her head. "Rick's a little under the weather today. I told him not to come in."

"Does he need anything?" B.T. asked. "China and I would be happy to deliver anything to him that he needs."

Magda smiled. "That would be right nice of you, B.T." Their eyes locked, and once again China saw the connection shoot back and forth. She couldn't believe that looks like that could be so tangible. She read about them in romance stories (which, for the most part, she couldn't stand). She saw the looks at weddings. But she never really saw them in real life. She rocked back on her heels and shoved her hands into her rear pockets. Watching this show left her speechless.

Magda put her arm around B.T.'s shoulders, walking him toward the kitchen. "What does B.T. stand for?"

"Brian Thomas, ma'am." B.T. shot China a look she didn't get.

"Nice name. Too bad you have to shorten it."

B.T. straightened up, and China knew it meant he was about to change identities. He leaned forward as if to tell Magda a secret. His hair fell even lower over his eyes. In a voice reminiscent of a cop show, he said, "I'm part of the secret witness program. I can never reveal my true identity. It could cause me great danger."

Magda threw her head back and laughed heartily. "Oh, you do go on now, don't you?"

She moved behind the food preparation table spread with mounds of unpeeled carrots and bunches of celery on one side. More mounds of cut and peeled carrots and celery lay on the other. Off to one corner sat a pile of celery hearts, bushy and furry. B.T. grabbed one and popped it underneath his nose like a mustache. In a low, masculine voice, he demanded, "You MUST pay the rent!"

Then he popped it on the top of his head. In a high, feminine voice, he cried, "I can't pay the rent!"

"You MUST pay the rent!"

"I can't pay the rent!"

"You MUST pay the rent!"

"I can't pay the rent!"

Then he dangled the celery from his chin, bushy side facing down like a beard. "I'LL pay the rent!" came an authoritative voice.

The celery landed on the top of his head again. "My HERO!"

"Rats!" said the mustached villain. "Foiled again!"

China laughed so hard, her sides hurt. Magda wiped underneath her eyes with her all-purpose apron.

B.T. put the celery in his mouth and started to munch. "Okay, Maggie, put me to work. Do you want me to peel or cut?"

"Oh, peel, please!" Magda shoved the peeler at him.

China went to the back room to get bowls for the finished stalks. She couldn't help but think about this creature who sat at the prep table peeling away like mad and making outrageous comments the whole time. "Help me!" he cried in a tiny voice. "I'm being skinned alive." Magda's chuckle rolled out in a continuous stream.

B.T.'s presence brought such a funny feeling inside. Kind of like peace dancing. China paused at the doorway and whispered, "Dear God, would it be okay if B.T. and I got to be good friends? I don't know if I've ever found such contentment with anyone before."

CHAPTER FIVE

"CABIN ASSIGNMENTS! COME AND GET YOUR free cabin assignments." Deedee marched into the kitchen, her clipboard held officiously in front of her. "Now," she announced, tapping the clipboard with the tip of her finger, "Mr. B.T. whatever your last name is. I would like to present you with your cabin assignment, if you would be so kind as to give me your name."

"Oh, he can't do that," China said quite seriously.

"And why not?" Deedee asked, drumming her fingers on the stack of papers.

Magda spoke up, dropping the last of the carrots into the bowl. "He's part of the victim witness program. To reveal his identity could mean certain death."

B.T. nodded his solemn agreement.

Deedee opened her mouth, pointed at B.T. with her official cabin assignment pen, then put it back.

"Close your mouth, dear," Magda said quietly. "You might land a bug or two."

B.T. snatched his fingers in the air as if catching a fly midflight and popped it into his mouth.

"They're quite tasty, you know, Maggie dearest. Perhaps the Deeds enjoys such flavorful nourishment." His eyes searched the air, and he snatched another invisible fly from it. "Care for a taste?"

"Of course," China answered, opening her mouth and closing her eyes. B.T. pretended to pop it in her mouth. China smacked her lips. "You are so right. It is quite delicious."

Deedee tossed her clipboard on the prep table and hopped up on the edge of it. "All right, all right. You win."

Magda motioned with her knife. "Off the table, Deedee. I want to feed my kids good, clean food."

Deedee slid off the table. She pointed at B.T.'s newly bandaged thumbs. "What happened to you?"

B.T. shrugged. "It's no big deal. I peeled my thumbs instead of the carrots a couple times."

Deedee shivered.

China shook her head. "There was blood everywhere. We had to remove all sharp objects from around him."

"Thomas," B.T. said out of the blue.

Deedee looked at him strangely. "Excuse me?"

"My last name is Thomas."

Deedee snatched a carrot stub from the garbage pile and chucked it at him. B.T. caught it in his hand and chucked it back. Deedee had looked away, and it caught her square in the side of the head. "Jubbah!" B.T. shouted triumphantly.

Magda stopped rinsing the knife and turned slowly to look at B.T. "Did you say a bad word?"

B.T. clutched his hands in front of him, squirming like a little boy. "No, ma'am."

"Then what did you say?"

"Jubbah," three voices chorused.

Magda shook her head and went back to washing her knife. They could hear her muttering a soft, "Jubbah," over and over under her breath as if she were trying it out to sift some distant memory.

"Well?" B.T. finally said, looking straight at Deedee.

"Well what?"

"I told you my last name. What's the assignment?"

Deedee flipped through her pages. "Brian Thomas?" She stared at the page. Held it up to the light. Squinted at it. Stuck the pen in her mouth, her lips puckering all around it. "It says here . . . " Her voice drifted off. She stared at the clipboard again. "It says . . . but it can't be right."

China stomped over and snatched the clipboard from her hand. "It says, 'Brian Thomas, Sparrow cabin.'" She tucked the clipboard back into Deedee's hands. "What's the big deal about that?"

"It's the cabin reserved for special guests. It's a single, China. He's all alone."

B.T. let an enormous amount of air escape as a gigantic sigh. "It's all out in the open. I might as well tell you."

Three pairs of eyes watched him, waiting for his terrible secret.

"I can see my reputation has preceded me."

Three heads nodded, silently encouraging him to speak.

B.T. slapped his forehead. "See? I knew! I knew this would happen." He turned away from them, wagging his head, staring at the ground. He paced back and forth. "I knew it, I just knew it," he muttered over and over.

China lost her patience, "What? Would you just let us in on this?"

"You promise you won't hate me?"

"We promise," Deedee and China said together.

"What's there to hate?" Magda said in her consoling voice. "Everyone has done things they are ashamed of. We are all children of sorrow coming to the Kingdom of Light."

"Okay, okay," B.T. said, holding up his hands, but still not making eye contact with them. "I'm . . . " He bit his lip and spun away. "Oh, I simply can't tell you!"

"Tell us," China said, her voice ready to explode.

"They put me in a cabin alone . . . " He let his voice trail off and sound as if sobs were about to begin. "Because I can't control my impulses to . . . to . . . "

China and Deedee held their breath.

" . . . say stupid words! Gyro! Schlockmeister! Nuncapative! Fungoid! Furculum!" B.T. spun around and around, clutching his head. "See? I can't stop! Zaibatsu! Pfeffernuss! Somebody, please help me stop! It's out of control! I'm addicted!"

The three stared at him, then Deedee broke. "You are an *idiot*, B.T.! You are a total idiot!" She grabbed a handful of carrot peelings from the trash and started after him.

China looked for something to get him with and snagged a wet dishtowel. Hissing and snapping the towel, she went on a rampage.

But a strange sound stopped them in their tracks. At first it sounded like a hiccuping growl. Then it grew to a spitting and hacking until it erupted with the strangest laughter they had ever heard. Magda rolled back and forth on her stool, the laughter exploding from the inner depths of her soul. She waved at them and sucked air in so hard it sounded like an old man's earsplitting snore. When she finally came up for air, she waved her hand at B.T. "You do beat all, child."

Deedee bonked B.T. over the head with her clipboard. "Okay. Spill the guts. Why are you alone?"

B.T. paused, letting his hair fall back over his eye. "I requested it."

Something about the way he said it shut Deedee up. China didn't want to push any further either.

"Oh my!" Magda exclaimed. "Dinner starts in one hour. Either you guys get busy in here or get out. I need to find my kitchen help and get them organized."

B.T. went up to Magda and looked down at her, holding his wayward hair so Magda could see both eyes. "I really should stay and help. But I should also go set myself up in my cabin. Can I help another time?"

Magda wrapped her arms around him. "Of course.Thanks for peeling the carrots."

The three walked to B.T.'s white Ford Bronco to get his stuff and help him carry it to the cabin.

"Nice car," Deedee said, her brows raised in approval.

"Yeah," B.T. said, obviously not wanting to talk about it any further. "Okay, let's get this junk outta here."

"I'll carry the guitar," China offered.

"It's very heavy," said B.T.

Deedee waved at him. "She's stronger than she looks. She can beat anyone in an arm wrestling match."

B.T.'s eyebrows went up. "Really?"

China blushed and shook her head. "Deedee, I don't want a repeat of what happened last time."

B.T. held the guitar, not letting it loose into China's grip. "What happened?"

"Nothing."

"The boy she beat locked her in the walk-in refrigerator."

B.T. nodded. "Sounds appropriate."

"He left her there for hours and didn't intend to tell anyone."

B.T. frowned and looked with deep concern at China. "That's not appropriate. Are you okay?"

"Okay in body, a little damaged in spirit."

B.T. let go of the guitar. He handed Deedee a satchel of papers, and he removed a giant suitcase.

"I didn't know you played the guitar," Deedee said.

The smile that broke over B.T.'s face seemed awfully broad for such a simple statement. "I fiddle with it every once in a while."

At the door to the cabin, B.T. made the girls promise they would meet him for dinner.

The girls looked at each other and then nodded. "Okay."

"Zareba. That'll be great."

"Zareba," the girls said as if it were good-bye.

⤴

The girls wove in and out of lost-looking campers as they hurried to change clothes and cancel dinner at the Kierseys'. "What do you make of that?" Deedee asked.

China felt like she was coming down off some kind of high. The further she got from the cabin, the more she felt like she had been cast under a spell.

"He's got some pretty bizarre energy," Deedee said.

China nodded. "He's really different than anyone I've ever known." She walked a few more steps.

"He's really crazy," said Deedee.

"Yeah. In a Robin Williams kind of way. So fast. So witty. So quick to change characters."

"I wonder if that's what Robin Williams was like as a kid."

"*I* wonder if that's why he's in a cabin by himself. If he really annoys people with his gags."

Deedee shook her head. "I can't imagine anyone being annoyed with his gags. He does them at just the right moment."

They walked in silence as they considered this whirlwind in a body.

"There's something about this guy that seems fishy," China said. "I wonder if he's who he says he is."

"Why wouldn't he be?"

"I don't know. But something's weird. I can't put my finger on it."

"He sure charmed Magda," Deedee said, as if that would be some sort of credential.

China sighed. "I hate to admit it, but there's something about him that makes me want to be around him every second." She laughed. "I'm sure he really wouldn't want to be with me."

Deedee hopped around in front of China and started walking backward. Her sleeveless flannel shirt flapped open, revealing the white T-shirt beneath. "I think you're falling in love with him."

China stuck her tongue out. "No way! You always think everyone is falling in love."

"But you are. It's written all over your face."

China rubbed her face with her hands, scrubbing it hard. "Is that better?"

Falling back into step with China, Deedee leaned her

head toward her. "Am I right or am I right?"

"You're wrong."

"You don't fool me."

China shook her head. "Really, I think you hit on it before. Maybe I've found the friend I've always wanted."

Deedee stopped dead. "Thanks a lot! What am I? A lump of burned marshmallow?"

China grabbed Deedee's arm. "You know very well I meant GUY friend, you dweeb." She sighed. "You don't have to worry, though. It will never happen."

"Why not?"

"Once he takes a good look at those gorgeous camp girls, we're history."

CHAPTER SIX

CHINA HAD FORGOTTEN HOW EELAPUASH smelled when you entered through the main door rather than through the kitchen. Robust smells of meat roasting in some sort of dark gravy. The smooth, thick smell of whipped potatoes with a yellow pool of melted butter floating on the top. Sweet Jell-O. Yeasty rolls.

She hung on to one of B.T.'s arms and Deedee clung to the other as B.T. swaggered into the milieu of kids.

Staring again at his odd outfit, Deedee poked him in the ribs. "Why are you wearing these stupid clothes?"

"To be different," B.T. hissed. "Now, shush! I don't want to draw attention to us."

A snort escaped China. "You have two females dangling like earrings from your elbows. You're wearing shades, your hair pulled back in a stubby ponytail, a fake mustache . . . "

"A weird suit coat with patched elbows," Deedee added.

"And you think no one is going to pay attention?"

"Remember, my name is Dale Robbins."

"Yes, Dale," China drawled. "We won't forget."

Dale steered his "appendages" toward the head table where Kemper sat with the girls' dean, the camp nurse, and the musicians, the Fong brothers.

"Yo, ladies!" Kemper boomed. "You recover yet from your wild ride this morning, China?"

The morning seemed like years ago. Had it only been a few hours since China had hated this crazy person at her side? Life simply happened too fast. She'd have to figure out some way to make it slow down. A small seed of hope grew in her that B.T., might really start to think of them as friends. She thought about saying something to dig at B.T. but then decided to tell the truth. "Actually, it was rather fun."

B.T.'s head swiveled so fast, his shades fell crooked across his nose. A lightning-fast hand pushed them into place and disappeared again into the pocket of the tweed jacket.

Kemper put out his hand to shake B.T.'s. "I'm really sorry I didn't realize . . . "

Instead of catching Kemper's hand, B.T. landed a finger on his lips to interrupt Kemper's sentence. Then B.T. stuck his hand in Kemper's. "Hi. I'm Dale Robbins."

Kemper chuckled. He motioned to the others at the table. "This here's Dale Robbins. I'm sure you'll see more of him later."

The metal chairs made horrible thumping sounds as they were dragged across the linoleum. Deedee leaned toward her escort. "B.T. . . . "

"Dale," B.T. corrected her.

"Dale," Deedee said, trying her hand at the drawl he asked them to use. But hers sounded more like her words were falling through her nose. "Why, oh why don't you want to sit at a table with some of the other campers? You will never meet anyone like this."

"Just give me time to warm up, sweetheart. I'm a little shy goin' into new places."

Kemper said the prayer, and the food appeared shortly after. By the end of the meal, the whole head table was talking in various renditions of Southern drawls. The group erupted in laughter so many times, people started to come up to ask what was so funny.

Without thinking, China automatically stacked and scraped the dishes. When they stared at her whirlwind activity, she shrugged. "Habit, I guess. It comes from working in the kitchen five days a week." She scooped up as much as she could carry and walked into the kitchen. Without dumping the dishes for someone else to take care of, she loaded them directly into the dish-washer racks.

"Show me how," came a voice behind her.

B.T. stood there, his own arms full, his mustache

starting to peel away on one side. China showed him the blue sterilizing silverware solution and where to find more dish racks for the dirty utensils he juggled in his arms.

"Going to the meeting?" he asked when they had finished.

"Don't know. Deedee doesn't usually like to go."

"Why not?"

"She's bored with all the God talk. She's heard it for so long, it doesn't mean anything anymore."

"She seems to like God enough."

"She does. But the words don't interest her anymore. I don't really know what to do about it."

B.T.'s next words surprised her. "Don't force it. I'm sure she'll come around."

"I wasn't worried."

B.T. took off his shades. "I'm sorry. I didn't mean to butt in or anything. I just didn't want you to feel like you had to go to the meeting with me. I've kind of made you guys stick around with me long enough. I should probably face this one alone."

"We don't do anything we don't want to. Well, most of the time. That's one of the great joys of being in a place like this. The only schedule we have is work, and that's not too demanding."

Deedee burst through the kitchen doors. "I thought Magda must have thrown you in her prison. Come on. The meeting's about to start."

"I didn't think you'd want to go," China said.

"Kemper said he's got a surprise for us. He said we HAVE to go."

B.T. slammed on his sunglasses with a groan.

China put her hands on her hips. "I don't like Kemper's surprises." She turned to B.T. "He has this way of really grossing us out."

"He promised it wasn't like that. He said we'd really like it."

China studied Deedee. "I guess if he convinced you, it's probably okay." She paused. "But then, you might be sworn to secrecy. He might be using you to get me to go. And then he'll do something horrible to me."

"You aren't a camper anymore, China. He only does the truly gross things to campers."

"But he tries them out on us first."

"Not in front of everyone. Come on. You coming, Dale?"

A halfhearted nod was all they needed to drag him from the kitchen and up the trail to Sweet Pea Lodge.

"I have to sit in front," China reminded Deedee.

"I haven't forgotten. But maybe we should sit in back for B.T."

The girls turned to look at him. In a small voice, he said, "The front will be fine."

The first night of camp singing always was a little on the sparse side. The kids seemed afraid to cut loose. But by the end of the week they'd be shouting, swaying, and putting their whole selves into each word. Deedee tried getting into it and getting everyone else to join in. But everyone just stared at her and let the words come out like they were made of lead.

B.T. leaned over and whispered to China, "I thought she didn't like the meetings."

"She doesn't like the speakers. But she loves the singing."

Kemper leaped on stage, his mustache quivering with excitement. He mopped his brow with a Happy Birthday napkin. "Is everybody going to have a great week at camp?"

A pitiful, "Yeah!" came back.

"Oh, man! That was so sad. If you don't have more energy than that, you'll never make it through the lake games tomorrow. Let's try again! Is everybody going to have a great week at camp?"

"YEAH!" came a little louder.

"Okay, forget it. I know something that will bring you to life. A few of you suspect, because you've been coming to me on the sly saying you saw something. Or you think you saw something. I didn't really answer you then. But I'm answering you now. What you saw was no illusion. What you saw was no clone or copycat. Yes, you saw the real thing."

Shrieks and excited chatter exploded like hot pop-corn in various spots throughout the room. B.T. sank lower in his chair and pulled the rubber band from his hair. He shook his head forward, hiding his face behind his hair. The sunglasses came off, as did the mustache.

"We are so privileged this week to welcome as our special guest musician the star of television's hit comedy *Family Squabbles*. Best known as Johnny Foster!"

A wild, chaotic burbling of sound cartwheeled in the room, drowning Kemper's final words. China and Deedee looked around B.T. at each other and shrugged their shoulders. "Did you know about this?" China asked Deedee. Deedee shook her head.

B.T. took a deep breath, then stood and put on his killer smile. He faced the crowd and waved with both hands over his head.

Deedee grabbed his tweed jacket. "Sit down, you nut. You're embarrassing me!"

China gulped, trying to keep her stomach down. Dumbfounded, she couldn't move. B.T. slipped out of his jacket and winked at Deedee. He moved on to the stage with the assurance of a star.

"Hi," B.T. said to the crowd. "You can just call me B.T."

A scream came from somewhere in the back. "I can't believe it! Johnny Foster HERE!?"

China's hope of friendship died that very instant. No TV star would give her the time of day.

Kemper raised his hands and made motions for them to quiet down. "Hey, guys! Yo! Chill down."

The crowd was talking and couldn't shut up. Couldn't

contain the excitement of having the hottest teen TV star right at their own camp.

Deedee put her fingers to her teeth and whistled. The crowd quieted momentarily.

Holding the microphone he had never had to use before, Kemper bellowed into it. "Quiet or I'm sending him home."

A pin dropped. And everyone heard it.

"B.T. here is coming to share his incredible music talent. And he'll be here the whole week. Everyone will get a chance to talk to him. He'll be on a team and he'll be a part of camp as long as everyone treats him with respect. NO autographs. He wants to be treated like just another kid. Okay? Don't disappoint us."

Leaping down from the stage, Kemper dropped himself into the seat next to the girls. "You guys have been so great to treat him normal," Kemper said.

Shock had still not worn off either face. "But we didn't know," Deedee whispered back.

"You didn't recognize him?"

For the second time that day, Deedee reminded him, "We don't watch television, silly."

A grin split Kemper's face. "Does it make any difference now that you know?"

Both girls wagged their heads, although China knew it made a huge difference. The possibility of friendship was as remote as winning a million-dollar lottery. At that moment, it seemed a circus broke loose inside her.

At once excited, happy, crazy, and chaotic.

I've been with a TV star and didn't even know it? He held my hand! She thought.

Clowns flipped somersaults in her stomach. Trapeze artists flew through her heart. Elephants stomped around the edges. Tigers and lions roared ferociously, bringing terror into the fun, warning her to stay away from him. It was as if she could break out into wild laughter and run screaming at the same moment. The circus began to collide in confusion.

What now? Will we still talk to him? Should I try and act . . . and act . . . how should I act?

A thread of sweet music wound its way into the melee and began to entice China's thoughts away from the mess. She lifted her gaze to the stage. B.T. perched on a stool picking the guitar strings (obviously an old friend), his soul lost in the song he sang. China had never heard it before.

Next to her, Deedee whispered. "He's really good."

When he finished, silence hung in the air. Then, as if cued to respond in unison, the crowd shattered the silence with cheers, stomps, and whistles.

B.T. came back from wherever he had gone, looked right at the girls, and winked.

The wink snapped China back into herself. She forgot it was Johnny Foster on stage. She lifted her chin and stuck her tongue out at him. Then she elbowed Deedee. "Let's get him. Let's get him good."

CHAPTER SEVEN

A WORD OF KEMPER'S TALK LANDED IN China's preoccupied brain every so often. But only a word. When the meeting was over, she still sat as if she were thumbing through private thoughts. In between fighting off scary thoughts of the real B.T., she tried to recall each prank she or her family had ever participated in or heard of. She tried mixing them, brainstorming wildly, but none seemed quite right. The punishment for B.T. must be precise and perfect . . . but not humiliating. Just enough to get him back for not letting her and Deedee know why people stared at them so oddly when they returned from riding and for using them to hide his identity.

Actually, she wasn't certain he *had* used them—if his desire to be with them was just to keep away from hordes of pestering fans (*Ahh, am I mosquito repellent now?*) or if he really liked them.

"Wake up!" Deedee hovered over her, arms crossed, her slender face wearing an amused smirk. "Let me in on what's going on in there." Deedee tapped China's head.

China shook the cobwebs from her brain. On stage B.T. was surrounded by an impermeable wall of kids.

"C'mon," Deedee said, grabbing China's arm. "We've gotta go help Magda."

On the way to the watermelon feed, China told Deedee what she was thinking.

"You're right," Deedee agreed. "None of those jokes are good enough for that twerp."

"Do you think he did it on purpose?" China asked.

Deedee wagged her head, her thick, braided hair brushing China on the cheek. "I've known too many of these famous people. Crud. Dad has had so many people over for dinner that we've stopped thinking of them as special. As a matter of fact, I don't even know if we ever thought they were special. It was just another person coming for dinner. Some of them glory in the recognition they get. Some of them hide because they hate crowds. And some of them simply act like a normal person. They seem oblivious to the commotion they cause."

"So you don't feel wierd about this?"

"Not that B.T. is on TV or anything. I feel weird that he didn't tell us."

The cool night air washed over China. Pungent pine filled every breath. The insects chirruped, making it sound like the stars actually twinkled.

Magda gave each girl a quick hug, then assigned them a table to slice melons. "Don't make the slices too thick the first time around," she instructed.

China enjoyed passing the juicy fruit to eager campers. Magda made them wear name tags that read, "HI! My name is . . . " Some of the kids teased China as if her name were fake. "Hi!" one said. "My name's Afghanistan."

"Hi! My name is Bolivia."

"And I'm her friend Peru."

"Hey!" said one chubby boy. "We must be related! My name's Mongolia."

Magda, at the table next to China, chuckled continuously as if it were the motor that kept her running. "I love these kids," she said over and over. "I surely do. They keep a woman young and laughing."

China glanced at her between slices and smiled. Magda looked into the crowd and her whole face changed. There was a look about her when she was swept magnificently away on the tide of some young man's concern about her. China supposed it was a look her son used to receive when he brought home a particularly good grade or a drawing he had made for her. Or some music he composed. She wore the look now. China didn't even have to look up to know who must be approaching the table.

B.T. somehow seemed to have adopted the expression of a loved son, the only time he showed some vulnerability. "Maggie!" he cried, seemingly oblivious to the stream of girls who followed. He moved around the

table and hugged Magda, watermelon-stained apron
and all.

Feeling as though she were intruding, China turned
away and began hawking watermelon. "My watermelon
slices are bigger!" she called.

"Mine are sweeter!" Deedee said, holding up a large,
dripping piece.

"I'm sorry, you guys. I hope you'll forgive me." B.T.
stood in front of them, his adoring fans at a safe distance behind him. "I really didn't mean to hurt you or
anything."

"You didn't hurt us," Deedee insisted.

"But we are a little miffed," added China.

"Speak for yourself," said Deedee.

"You said you wondered why he did it."

"So? That doesn't mean I'm miffed. I'm curious."

Finished with their little conversation, they both
looked at B.T., hoping for an explanation.

"Hey!" a big, beefy guy said, pushing his way through
the group. "I want some more watermelon. Quit hogging the line!" As soon as he saw who stood at the
table, he shrank back like a bigger bully was waiting to
deck him.

"Go ahead!" B.T. said, gesturing to the table. "I *am*
hogging the line." With that, he turned and walked
away, looking somewhat like a mother hen with all her
little chicks scurrying and chattering in a fuzzy cloud
behind her.

As they passed out seconds of watermelon, Deedee asked, "Are you still mad?"

"I don't know that I ever was. Confused maybe." China thought a moment, then the evil grin lit her face again. "But I still want to get him back."

"Doesn't what he said mean anything?"

How could China let Deedee know that it meant too much? That one look from his piercing blue eyes affected her so much that she had forgotten to breathe. She didn't like that. She had to keep up some kind of protection. People who could crawl inside you were experts at hurting you—without even knowing it. She knew that no one important would ever truly like her. Once they found out who she was, they'd see she was plain white bread. Vanilla. Nothing terribly interesting.

"'Course what he said means something. But it doesn't mean we can't put a little excitement in his life."

"So what's your plan this time?"

"Don't know yet. We need to observe him a little longer."

                                    ⁂

In bed that night, China lay still, unable to sleep. "Deeds," she whispered, "are you awake?"

The lump in the bed next to her made no sound.

Rolling over, China hunkered down in the sleeping bag and shoved her head under the pillow. She felt sad somehow. Sad that the day was over.

She smiled to herself, warm, good feelings trickling down inside of her. Her smile grew bigger as she closed her eyes and pictured B.T.'s bewilderment at his horse dropping from underneath him. His good humor at being dumped in the water trough. His suave, way of carrying himself as a cowboy. His focused attention on Deedee's foot, oblivious to the fact that he had shoved China down the hill.

Every moment of the day reviewed itself in her mind—even the end moment. The one where he walked away from the melon tables, his new bevy of girls to choose from. *He won't want us anymore.* China thought. *He's got a whole camp of somewhere around a hundred girls to choose from. Every single one would count themselves lucky to be chosen as his.*

Her grandma Petey's words came back to her in a flash. "There's no one so different in this world that you are better than they are. Don't you ever forget that, China. And even more important, there's no one so different in this world that they are better or more special than you."

She squirmed, the pillow falling off her head. But B.T. was more special, wasn't he? She and Deedee didn't have crowds of people wanting to be their friends. They didn't have crowds of people following them or screaming when someone said their names. Or wanting them to write their names on scraps of paper. B.T. could choose . . . he didn't have to do anything he didn't want. B.T. had power . . . he probably had more money than most people would ever have in their entire lives. All this made him different enough to be more special. The crowds of people proved that. "Special" was proven by your volume of friends and the importance of your work. And most teens didn't even work!

Heavy thoughts weighed her down, deeper and deeper, until . . .

❧

The next morning Mr. Kiersey sat at the kitchen table finishing his coffee while poring over the newspaper. "The only time I wish we had a television," he muttered.

"What, Daddy?" Deedee asked, kissing the top of his balding head.

"The Olympics. I really miss watching the Olympics."

"And the World Series. And the Super Bowl."

Mr. Kiersey sighed, putting down his empty mug. "Those too."

"You wouldn't have time to watch the Olympics anyway."

"I know."

China sidled up to Mr. Kiersey. She put her arm around him and thought about kissing his cheek, then changed her mind. He smelled of soap and the tang of something citrus.

Mr. Kiersey pushed back his chair. "Nope! You girls must have a proper hug each morning." He doled out his strong embraces and headed for the sink with his mug. "Oh. Here's a note from Kemper. He called. Wants you two to keep score at the lake for the relay. You can wear your suits if you want and swim afterward."

The girls exchanged a pleased look. "It's better than the mud pit," China said happily.

Deedee grabbed her dad's arm. "Daddy? Why didn't you tell us about B.T. coming up?"

Mr. Kiersey moved back to the table and folded the paper, tossing it into the growing stack in the corner. "Didn't think of it."

"If he's supposed to be so famous . . . "

"Actually, I'd never heard of him, so I really didn't think about it."

"Isn't it unusual to let a seventeen-year-old kid stay in his own cabin? Or even to be part of the program?"

"You still questioning your old dad, Deedee?" A note of irritation crept into Mr. Kiersey's voice. "I'm the dad. I'm the boss of the camp. Why must you question every decision I make?"

"I . . . " Deedee's eyes narrowed. Her hands started to roll into little fists. Instead of letting the explosion out, she ran down the hall to her room.

Her head buried deep in the pantry, China pretended to be looking for the cereal. She heard Mr. Kiersey sigh and leave the house, closing the door a little harder than necessary.

CHAPTER EIGHT

MOVING SILENTLY THROUGH THE CLOTS OF kids on the shores of Little Bear Lake, China tried to keep her rebellious thoughts in check. She kept scolding them that they couldn't tell her to look for B.T. But they did anyway. She tried to reason with them. *He's out of my league as a friend. He's out of my league as a human being. Look. Every connection you felt from him to me and Deedee was just a way for him to break the ice, to get used to a new situation where he couldn't possibly feel comfortable.*

But her head still swiveled, searching the crowd. Her heart still hoped. Sometimes she hated herself—hated the lack of control over her stupid body that reacted to every single emotional thought.

Walking with China, Deedee seemed as calm and unaffected as ever.

When they reached Kemper, China focused all her attention on him and his instructions.

"The first relay is a canoe relay—no paddles. They have to use their hands and paddle around the buoy and back. Your job is to watch and make sure your team follows the rules. China, you're in charge of the Black Widows. Deedee, you're in charge of the Locusts. After that, we have the Around the Lake relay. In this one, rather than assign you to a team, I'm going to assign you to a station. Deedee, you are to stand on the far side of the lake to be sure the players properly form the caterpillar walk—you remember how to do that?"

Deedee nodded.

"And China, you be at the bottom of the slide to make sure the sliders tag their teammates' canoe before they paddle across the lake. After that, return to your team posts and you'll hear the instructions for the other games."

The girls trotted to their official posts after getting their official whistles from the official lifeguard from his official stand. "I feel very official now," Deedee said, her whistle poised between her teeth.

"My team's better," China said with a haughty look.

A stirring in the crowd caught China's attention. Her heart started to beat faster before she saw what caused the murmuring. It was as if that connection in her was electrified the moment the source entered anywhere nearby. She pinched her arm hard, hoping that would stop the ridiculous surge inside her. Then she had to laugh. B.T. wore red swim trunks with a red cross insignia on one leg. Zinc oxide painted his nose a glaring white. Ultra-cool shades covered his eyes. On his head, he wore an old, beat-up straw hat like her grandmother Petey used to wear to putz around in her garden. From a distance, she couldn't quite make out what was going on with the upper half of his body. His arm muscles looked enormous. His torso rippled with Mr. World muscles. But wait. They didn't ripple at all. They seemed to stay still. Laughter rumbled through the crowd and erupted into gigantic proportions as he walked by.

"Oh, brother!" Deedee exclaimed. "He's got some kind of rubber body on!"

The closer he came, the better China could see what Hollywood can do. B.T.'s rubbery arms even had hair growing on them!

He had adopted a muscle-man swagger, his head nodding with every step. "Hello," he said, his voice deep and mellow. "Hello." He waved with a casual flip of his hand to no one and everyone. "You can relax now. You're all safe with me around."

Without any awe or pretense, Deedee marched right up to him and squeezed his rubber biceps. "Oh, Popeye!" she squealed. "You're my hero!" Fresh laughter surrounded them. Deedee batted her long eyelashes at him and he batted his right back. He took her hand, placed it in the crook of his arm, and began to swagger away. Everyone applauded.

Kemper's voice boomed over the bullhorn. "Places,

everyone! Gather in your teams. This includes you, too, Popeye."

The teams listened to the rules of the first game, then huddled to decide who would be the players in each part of the canoe relay.

At that moment, China wished she were Deedee. That she had the same guts as Deedee. The same casual air. The same belief that all people were the same and that famous people didn't mind if you pretended they were like someone you'd known forever.

B.T. whispered something and Deedee threw back her head and laughed, the sun glinting off her hair, a deep red color for which there was no name. Deedee had it all. A warm, loving family. Hair to die for. And the gift for making people feel comfortable and at home, no matter where they were.

A bleat from the bullhorn brought China back to her duties. Her heart, though, couldn't quite come to its senses.

The teams lined up across the beach. The whistle blew, the water filled with splashing campers pushing canoes ahead of them to get a good start. The Stink Bugs and the Scorpions dumped their canoes trying to get in. The Black Widows and the Locusts took off in the lead. Everyone quickly got caught up in the competi- tion—including China. She jumped up and down, screaming encouragement, her voice straining with the abuse. By the time the race was over, China was glad she had worn her suit underneath her T-shirt. All the splashing relayers managed to soak her, too.

Kemper announced the game a success. This meant no one drowned, no one was hurt, and almost everyone got wet.

Kemper nodded at China and Deedee, and they took off for their stations. As they jogged around Little Bear, Kemper bored everyone with the rules for the next relay.

China stopped beneath the twenty-five-foot-high slide. A sheet of water cascaded down the shiny steel surface, ending in a small waterfall off the foot of the slide. A cloud of spray emanated from the top of the slide, giving the impression it was a formidable mountain surrounded by mist. The kids had nicknamed it K-2. China thought it looked more like a metallic dragon's tongue ready to lap up the lake water.

Shouts and cheers sounded on the beach. The game had begun. China's post was third in the relay. The first task was for each team to successfully throw three syrup-soaked Nerf balls into a small basketball hoop worn on the chest of an unfortunate team member. Kemper had giggled when he told them no one ever made the baskets right away. Then the syrup-splattered person had to roll in the sand. Two new team members paddled a canoe to the foot of the slide. A third ran around the shore, slid down the slide, swam to tag the canoe, and then the canoe took off across the lake.

More team members waited there at Deedee's station to perform the caterpillar walk.

China's heart picked up speed again. *Stupid heart! It acts like my team is in on this. Or like I'm supposed to race.* She wondered if she'd ever be able to get it under her control. It didn't seem to care what the truth was. It reacted the way it wanted, when it wanted.

Screams and voice levels rising and falling were the measure of what was happening out of China's sight. A crowd split apart, probably to let someone roll to the lake. Splashing. A canoe was off. A runner headed toward her. "Come on", China said, urging the stranger on. The canoe reached the slide before the runner did. "Stink Bug," the runner called before climbing the four levels of ladder rungs to the top. He sucked in a deep breath before sailing down the slide. "WHOW!" he whooped when he came up sputtering for air. "It's COLD!" He swam furiously to the canoe and slapped it hard enough for China to hear.

The second and third runners came on each other's heels. "Black Widow," said one. "Scorpion," said the other. Two canoes waited impatiently. The boat occupants sat with their backs to the slide, dangling their hands in the water ready to paddle.

China watched each person climb, slide, splash, and slap.

Two more runners were on their way. A girl and . . . Popeye. He ran so stiffly and upright, his fat arms pumping in exaggerated motions. The girl who ran with him held her sides, hardly able to breathe right because laughter stole the air away.

Enjoying life at every turn. That's what he does! China thought. *That's what I want to learn.*

"Popeye" B.T. reached the slide first but bowed graciously, his arm gesturing toward the ladder. "Ladies first."

"Thank you!" the girl said. She lightly tripped up the ladder. At the top, she paused. "It's scary from up here."

"Why do you think I let you go first?" B.T. called up to her. "I wanted to see if you die. If you do, I don't go."

The girl's team screamed at her: "Go! Go! Go!" She sat down, held her nose with her right hand, and let go with the left.

"See you after lunch?" B.T. asked China, swinging himself up the first ladder.

"I work all afternoon in the kitchen."

B.T. winked at her and was gone. His feet lightly tapped the rungs. Higher and higher he went. China didn't realize she watched his every move until her neck started to hurt. She backed away from the slide in order to see him better. At the top, he pummeled his chest, a Tarzan yell echoing across the lake. He held on to the overhead bar, swinging himself into position. He swung forward, back, then forward, letting go.

"Yeowww!" he yelled, his arms straight up in the air. China imagined he rode roller coasters the same bold way. The final runners breathlessly came up behind her, telling her their team names.

"China," a husky voice said.

The whole beach had suddenly caught its breath. There were no more excited shrieks and cheers.

She looked up. B.T. was still there halfway down. His hands gripped the sides of the slide, and he sat sideways.

"What are you doing?" she scolded. "You're ruining it for your team."

"You've got to come help me." His voice was still husky, his face going white.

She cocked her head, looking carefully at him. "Are you joking?"

"No. I need you. Please."

China pushed aside the other runners who were already on their way up to the top. The icy mist stung her arms and coated her face. She sat at the top of the slide, trying to figure out what was wrong and what to do. Where she sat, the water was pure and clear. Below B.T., it was red.

"My toe got caught in the side here. I can't get it out. It's bleeding pretty bad."

"What can I do?"

"Come down here and pull it out while I hold on."

China shuddered. "If I slide to you, I'll crash into you."

"Turn off the water. That'll help."

China turned to the guys behind her. "Go down to the bottom and turn off the water." To B.T., she said, "Don't you want someone stronger—like this guy here—to help instead?"

B.T. shook his head. "There's a better chance a light person will do better. Besides," he looked straight into her eyes, "I want you."

She saw it in his eyes. She saw the truth in them. She saw the connection. She saw the words he didn't say: *I trust you.*

The water stopped, and China moved slowly down the slide. She planted her feet on the metal, grasping the sides as tightly as she could. She didn't want to go too fast. Didn't want to lose control. She inched forward. First the toes. Then the fingers. Then the toes. Then the fingers.

"Hurry! I don't know how long I can hold on."

It all seemed so ludicrous. The rubber muscles. The lifeguard trunks. The kids so quiet on the shore. Everyone watched, frozen. "Tell me this isn't happening," China said.

"This isn't happening," B.T. hissed. "The camera's up in the trees."

Without thinking, China looked up.

"Heh, heh, heh," B.T. laughed dryly. "Come on, China. I know you can do this without ripping my toe off."

"Thanks for the vote of confidence," China told him, still inching forward. When she reached the spot just above him, she checked out the situation. The only way she could do this was to get closer than would be terribly comfortable.

"It's okay," B.T. said. "I won't bite . . . " Then under his breath: " . . . too hard."

"Stop it," China said, trying not to laugh. She slipped her left leg behind B.T., glad for once she'd gotten terribly limber in order to gross her brother out by being able to do the splits. She curled her right leg into her body. She could feel B.T.'s breath on the back of her neck. She bent over, peering at probably the only spot on the entire slide where the metal gaped just big enough for a baby toe to slide in and get stuck.

"How in the world did you do this? You're supposed to slide with your feet together. Didn't your mother ever teach you anything?"

"I'm a teenager. I'm not supposed to listen to my mother."

China sighed and shook her head. "You're impossible."

"That's what Mom says."

"I wish I had two hands to do this, B.T."

"Just do it."

"It's going to hurt."

"I'm Popeye, remember? I can take anything."

Gently grabbing hold of B.T.'s foot, China closed her eyes to pull.

"Open your eyes, girl. I don't want you ripping my

toe off because you pulled the wrong way."

"Picky, picky." China bit her lip, holding it under her teeth as if it would help her do a better job. She pulled his foot toward her. She moved slowly, hoping it wouldn't stick. B.T.'s breath came in short gasps. A small sound almost like a whimper with macho attached caught in his throat. "Zarf! That hurts!" Then, the toe was free.

"Turn the water back on," B.T. shouted to the guys below. Then to China: "I'm not about to get stuck again."

The fresh water flowed around them.

"Now I know how a rock feels in the middle of a stream." B.T. attempted a smile, but it looked far more like a grimace.

"Now what?" China asked.

"I let go." And he was gone, a trail of blood streaking the delighted dragon's tongue. When he hit the water, China followed. When she surfaced, the teams all cheered.

Deedee waited at the bottom, Trina the nurse with her. She shook her head. "How do you do it, B.T.? First the atlasphere, then the horse. The horse more than once. Now this."

Hopping on to the grass and dropping into it, he looked up at her. "I don't have enough excitement in my life."

CHAPTER NINE

YOU'RE A HERO," DEEDEE TOLD CHINA during the family lunch. "Mom, you should have seen what she did. She deserves another one of Kemper's red crosses."

"I happened to be in the right place at the right time," China countered. "It would have been you if Kemper had reversed the stations."

"She was great, Mom."

Anna poked her chubby finger into her peanut butter and jelly sandwich. She looked at China, took her thumb out of her mouth, and said, "Hero." It came out sounding more like "hair-o."

"Man!" Deedee's little brother Adam said, shaking his head mournfully. "I wish I hadda been there. All that blood. Cool! Did it look cool, China?"

Joseph, one step younger than Adam, looked eagerly for China's answer.

"It was so cool," China said, looking from one to the other, "that I made your sandwiches with it."

Both boys looked between their bread slices at the

raspberry jelly. "Oh, this is so gross!" Adam exclaimed. Then he picked up his sandwich and ate a big bite.

Mrs. Kiersey shook her head and chuckled. "Thanks for encouraging them, China."

"Anytime, Mrs. Kiersey."

After lunch, China accompanied Deedee to the boat shack. "I'd rather go riding with B.T. than work all afternoon," Deedee said with a sigh. "How 'bout you?"

"And see another horse die? I don't have the heart for it."

Deedee punched her in the arm. "Really. What would you rather do? I know something's going on in that bizarre head of yours. I can see your mind working, but I don't know what it's saying."

China scuffed her feet in the dirt. The sun baked the top of her head, making her feel hot all over. Biting her lip, she looked up into the giant oak. She tried to pull something out of her thoughts, which were as jangled and interwoven as the branches of the ancient tree. But they all seemed so private. Naked little thoughts. She'd have to wait until she had clothes for them before she could show them off.

"Are you closing me out?" Deedee asked quietly.

China threw her arm around Deedee's neck. "No. I just can't figure out what my thoughts are quite yet."

They walked silently in the summer heat, trying to avoid the clouds of gnats hanging out in the shady spots.

China helped Deedee unlock the boats and get ready for the campers from all over the canyon who would come to rent the boats. She waved good-bye, feeling quite unable to speak.

The slide had a yellow ribbon blocking it off. No spray misted at its peak. Workmen were setting up a platform in order to get to the spot where B.T. caught his toe. China was glad the camp was so careful, but she figured there was no need to be. This could only happen to B.T. And *she* thought she was a disaster waiting to happen. He was far worse. Maybe that's why there was an instant connection with them. The little accident-prone kid inside each of them recognized one another.

The kitchen was the perfect place for China when thoughts she didn't understand came over her. There she found a loving Magda, who knew how to let people be themselves. Rick made the day lighthearted and fun. His singing of songs from old musicals let the mind rest from things it couldn't figure out. And this was one thing she really couldn't figure out. *But at least I'm in Rick's league. I'll never be in B.T.'s.*

Magda took one look at her and wrapped her in a Pillsbury Dough Boy hug. She whispered in her ear, "Don't worry about it, China honey. Whatever it is will work itself out."

China kissed Magda's soft cheek. "Thanks."

"I'll put you on back-room duty today, if you like."

China thought a moment. "I'd rather be where my thoughts can't take over. Out here would be better."

"How about working with Rick? Would that be okay?"

"The best."

Rick slid by on stockinged feet, his arms up, acting as if he were skating. He gave a little kick and turned in the air. "Another perfect triple lutz performed by . . . "

"I thought you were supposed to be sick."

"I recover fast. Come on. Come help me get the lasagnas made." He skated by the other way. "I could have daunced all night," he sang, his arms fluttering.

All the ingredients for the lasagnas were laid out on the prep table in industrial-size pots, pans, and bowls. Rick and China formed an assembly line, working closely together, their heads practically touching. China poured in the sauce and layered the noodles as Rick spooned in meat and sprinkled the cheese. They chatted happily about a zillion different things while, lasagna after lasagna was built and laid to rest in a shelved cart.

China adored Rick and his ability to make life fun. His ability to take a spoonful of sugar to help the medicine go down. His total assurance with himself. He didn't care who saw him being crazy. He enjoyed life, and you could enjoy it with him if you wanted. Around him, she relaxed. He was like a big brother, should be. Not like her own brother, Cam, who couldn't care less if she existed.

She and Rick had built a good friendship by working together. By sharing their dog, Bologna. They worked, playfully crashing their arms together, shoving and telling each other to "get out of the way."

But China noticed something. The heart connection seemed to be missing. It didn't mean they weren't friends. Or that they didn't share stuff. Or that they didn't like being together. There was definitely a difference between being with Rick and being with B.T. One she still couldn't quite figure out.

"Tell me about him," Rick said, interrupting her reverie.

Blushing, China thought maybe she had said something out loud. Maybe he could read her thoughts. "Who?"

"The TV star. I watch that show all the time. Not while I work here, of course. But during the winter. He's very funny. Got a good singing voice, too. I can never think of his name. I can only think of him as Johnny Foster."

"Brian Thomas. He goes by B.T."

"And? What's he like?"

Something different hovered about Rick. His eyes brightened beyond their regular brightness. His movements became sharper. Quicker. Not smooth and casual. "I suppose . . . " China's voice drifted off. She bit her lip and poured a ladle of spicy tomato sauce into the bottom of the baking pan. Her mind quickly thumbed through photographs of the day before. Of the morning in the sun, his blond hair golden. Almost blinding. His easy smile and laughter just under the surface, ready to come out at the least little excuse. His crazy sense of humor. The depth he kept hidden behind the fun.

"He's always an actor," she started. "Always being a different character. He's very good at it. Very spontaneous."

"I figured he had to have some of his television character in him. He's just too funny. Too natural."

"He's really nice, though."

"Stuck up?"

"Not at all."

The screen door slammed. "Sorry," a voice said. China felt chills up her spine. "Anyone home?"

Magda rushed by Rick and China. "What's her hurry?" Rick asked.

Magda came around the corner, the look once again taking over her whole face and even affecting her body. B.T. hobbled behind her, his right tennis shoe unlaced. His foot was fat, with the hint of an ace bandage poking out of a sock. His eyes met China's and something she couldn't define was in the look. She had to look away. "Rick," she said, using him as an excuse, "this is B.T."

Recognition had already taken Rick by surprise. He wiped his hand back and forth on his apron, then stuck it out to B.T. "We were just talking about you."

B.T. looked at China. She blushed again. "Oh, you

were? What terrible things did China tell you about me? I suppose she was telling you how I tried to kill her in the atlasphere. It couldn't have been anything nice."

"How's your foot?" Rick asked.

"Only eight stitches. I'm lucky I wasn't going faster or I'd be a nine-toed sloth right now."

"You're just a ten-toed sloth then, right?" China teased, then blushed. *Who do I think I am, teasing a TV star?*

"If I had a full foot, I'd kick you," B.T. teased back.

Rick kept talking, the stars still blurring his vision. "I see your show all the time—that is, when I'm not working here. You're really good."

A smile China hadn't seen before moved B.T.'s face. "I'm glad you enjoy it. That's what my job is—to make people laugh."

His voice changed, too. It sounded stilted and formal.

Rick stopped working and leaned on the prep table. "I'd like to know more about your music."

China took over Rick's work station and built the remaining three lasagnas by herself. Magda busied herself within hearing range, looking often and fondly at B.T.

"There's not much to tell," B.T. said, perching himself on the edge of the prep table. Both Rick and China threw Magda a look to see if she would say anything. But she only smiled.

"I love my music . . . it expresses how I feel inside. I don't have to be funny with my music. I can be myself."

"Do you write your own stuff?"

"Not the smarmy stuff they make me play on the show. I do write my own worship music. I don't usually tell people that. I want people to praise God, not me."

"Did you write those songs you sang last night?" China asked, amazed.

B.T. looked at her, startled, as if he'd forgotten she was there. "Yeah. But don't broadcast it." He smiled as he said it. She returned the smile and went back to her work.

"I only wish the network would let me do a few of my original things."

"Aren't they too Christian-y for the show?" Rick asked.

"Not all my stuff is worship music. I have some fun songs that talk about what's right without mentioning God. I wrote them specifically for the show, but the producers simply won't hear of it. They want Johnny Foster to be what they call 'real.' And let's face it. Brian Thomas is not anyone's picture of what teenagers are supposed to be like. Teen guys, especially, are supposed to be so wrapped up in girls they can't think of anything else except cars and sports."

"And that's not you, is it, B.T. honey?" Magda said.

China shot a glance at B.T. She wondered how he would tolerate being called honey. He simply smiled at

Magda and shook his head. "Sure I like cars. Sure I like sports. But I'm trying to figure out this God thing. I've been through enough rough times to know life isn't easy. It's my guess that knowing God and doing what he wants me to do is more important than those other things."

"What about girls?" Rick asked. "I suppose you have a lot of girlfriends."

China thought Rick looked about ready to drool.

"I could if I wanted. But I'm only seventeen. If the point of dating is to find a marriage partner, then I'd rather wait until I'm old enough to get married to start dating. Right now I'd rather find some real special girls to be true friends. The few times I dated, I was constantly wondering if they were with me because I had enough money to give them a good time or if it was because they liked being with me. No, for right now, I'm enjoying the possibility of friends." No one could miss the way he looked at China.

Turning away so no one could see her stupid face blush again, she put the last pan of lasagna on the cart and rolled it away. *He doesn't really think of me as a friend. He's probably just trying to be nice. Hmmph! What else is he supposed to say?*

CHAPTER TEN

B.T. SLAPPED HIS HANDS TOGETHER AND rubbed them. "Okay, Maggie, time to put me to work."

Rick's eyebrows raised so fast and high that China thought they might just land somewhere in his hairline and never return.

Magda put her hands on her ample hips and looked B.T. over closely. "You're a guest here. Guests don't work."

"This one does. Point me to an apron."

"You and China can make garlic toast. I'm putting China in charge of whipping the butter."

"I can do that," B.T. reassured her. "I'm stronger."

China pouted, sticking her tongue out at him. Rick came up behind her and put his arm around her shoulder. "She's plenty strong. She beat our prize kitchen worker at arm wrestling . . . and threw him out of the kitchen."

"So I heard," B.T. said, looking China over approvingly.

"It didn't happen like that . . . " China protested.

"China's strong enough," Magda interrupted.

91

"Besides, I don't trust you around those blades." She looked pointedly at his foot.

"Wise choice, I'm sure," B.T. said, laughing. "I'll unwrap."

Eight pounds of butter and several cloves of garlic were soon churning together in the Hobart. Armed with flat spreaders, the two began to spread the mixture over six hundred pieces of bread. "We're all pigs, aren't we?" B.T. mentioned.

"What's worse is how much we throw away."

"How come you don't make less, then?"

"It always seems that the one item you make less of is the item everyone wants more of. Besides, Magda says bread is the only thing all the kids eat. So if they don't like lasagna, at least they can fill up on bread. She's right. It's the one thing we never have to throw out much of."

"Don't you just love working here?" B.T. asked her as sounds of Rick singing "Somewhere Over the Rainbow" drifted through the kitchen.

"Yeah. Magda and Rick really make it fun. I think it would be boring with anyone else."

B.T. stopped mid-spread and stared at her. "You know, some people really have the knack for kindness. I think you've been especially gifted."

"I didn't mean you."

"Well, you're working with me now."

China shook her head. "I meant if I had another set of bosses."

B.T. swabbed another layer of butter on the bread. "I know. I just wanted to make you sweat."

China took a blob of butter from the table and dabbed his nose with it. "I'd get you worse, but I don't know you well enough."

"Maggie, am I doing this right?" B.T. asked her as she chugged by with a cartload of punch containers.

She stopped, checking out the sourdough bread slice he held in his hand. "A little less butter would be good, B.T. honey."

B.T. scraped some of the butter off until Magda gave her nodding approval. Then he picked up other prepared slices and started scraping some of the butter off them, too.

Magda wagged her head and clucked her tongue. "Now, don't get yourself carried away, B.T. You don't need to waste time going back over the old ones."

"You sure?" B.T. asked, a slice of bread in his hand, the knife poised to scrape.

Magda chuckled. "I'm sure."

For the next few pieces, B.T. carefully spread the same amount of butter on each one. Finally, China slapped his arm. "B.T.! Give me a break! This isn't chemistry class. Just slap a little butter on and get on with it."

"I want to be sure it's right."

"Whatever help you give is more than we expected anyway. If you can't enjoy it, then don't do it. You're making me crazy."

After ages of spreading butter, they put the bread on trays and slid them into the ovens. After the bread was toasted, they put twelve slices in each basket and then put the baskets on the warmer. The kitchen fell away as they got deeper and deeper into conversation. Their work became a pattern of place, slide, toast, and basket. They didn't have to concentrate to pay attention to their task. They didn't realize they worked so well together. They didn't notice Rick, Magda, and other kitchen workers moving in and out about them. The only thing they realized was that in some strange way they had so much in common.

The entire world, it seemed, watched, judged, and reported every move B.T. made. How he chewed, how he walked, how he shopped, how he interacted with his friends. He never knew when something he'd done would appear on the front of a tabloid in supermarket checkout lines.

A whole different world watched every move China made. How she acted, if she obeyed her parents, if she was a good example to the world for missionaries. Everything she did was reported in prayer letters sent out to supporters all over the United States and Canada. If she made a mistake or rebelled, or did something stupid, she became one of the prayer requests for the month.

B.T. spent most of his time in a different culture. Sure, it was America, California even. But Hollywood lived by its own standards, rules, and customs. B.T. was so used to it, he often forgot that real life was quite a bit different. He spent 12-14 hours a day living with facades and false identities. To come out of that was sometimes a shock.

China had the culture of Guatemala to contend with. A conflicting past and present inside of one country. Ancient customs clashing and merging with modern progress, yet nothing was ever quite the same as the States.

Both had different languages to deal with. Both were lonely in their struggles to understand their place in the world. Both had to live by the standards and expectations of others, so they didn't have a chance to figure out what they would do and be if left alone.

"That's why I like camp so much," China told him. "Only a few people know I'm an MK, so I can pretty much act like I want. No one's staring at me, watching my every move."

B.T. heaved a big sigh. "That's why I like being with you and Deedee. To you guys, I am just 'B.T. the idiot.'"

China blushed with embarrassment. "I'm so sorry."

"Please don't be sorry. I loved being called an idiot."

"You *are* strange."

B.T. popped the oven door open and removed a hot tray. China replaced it with a cool one and closed the door.

"Is that why you didn't tell us who you were?"

B.T. leaned on the warming table. A half-smile crept on to his face. "I thought maybe I had entered the Twilight Zone or something. It's so rare that people like me for me and not because I'm a TV star or rich . . . " His voice faded. He turned away, letting his hair fall over his face.

"What's it like to be on TV?" China asked.

"It's not as glamorous as everyone thinks." It took six trays' worth of toasting time for him to tell her about the long hours, the many times the whole script was re-written in one night, so the cast had to memorize their new parts all over again—and fast. He told her about having school on the set and having to learn camera positions more quickly than the adults. While the adults ran through the script, he was being tutored. "Most of my friends are adults—people I meet on the set. It's hard, hard work."

"Do you like it?"

"I love it. Sometimes I get frustrated and tired and lonely and I think of quitting. But every time we put the show together in front of the audience and hear the genuine laughter, it becomes worth it all over again. It is SO much fun."

Deedee seemed to appear out of nowhere, and China suddenly became aware of her surroundings again. Rick was in the middle of "Get Me to the Church on Time," and she realized she hadn't heard him from the beginning.

"Are we going to eat together or not?" Deedee demanded, arms crossed and tapping one toe.

China and B.T. must have looked blank or lost, or both.

"Hello? Anyone home?"

B.T. snapped to attention, saluting Deedee. "Yes, SIR! The kitchen crew is ready, SIR!"

Deedee put her arm through his. "Let's go," she said in a soft, soothing, motherly tone. "I'll have you taken away to the nuthouse in a little bit. But I can't let them take you away on an empty stomach."

This time B.T. maneuvered Deedee to the nearest table filled mostly with guys. China followed, still in the dreamy state of television studios and trying to imagine the world B.T. had shared with her. She watched the different B.T. around all these kids. She felt a small, quiet satisfaction that she knew a B.T. none of these other guys knew. She only felt sad Deedee hadn't had the chance to know him, too. The flame of hope began to flicker to life again. *Maybe we can be friends.* She swallowed hard, as if trying to swallow away the thought and not get her hopes up too much.

Within minutes after Kemper's prayer, B.T. had them all talking like space aliens. They had renamed the food to fit their space theme, and everyone laughed so hard they could hardly eat.

Afterward, B.T. pulled the girls aside and said, "We'll have to do this again sometime. Only, without the murmuring crowds."

"No one in the world talks like you," Deedee told him.

"I should hope not. It would be totally frightening."

China had promised Magda that if they ate dinner with the other kids, they would come back and finish the job that was usually done during dinner.

China loved working with B.T. He smiled and teased her often. She laughed and teased him back. And for a while, she forgot that he was Johnny Foster, superstar. He was just B.T. A new friend. And she knew she didn't have to worry or wonder if he was like the guys Deedee had told her about who seemed like the only reason they came to camp was for a quick romance. They didn't want any hassles of having a steady girlfriend. No ties. But they wanted to grab as much physical affection as they could before they left camp, promising to call and write. They probably never did.

Deedee told her of girls who were just as bad. "Either way, it's a game. And it's certainly no fun if they are playing you and you don't know it. You should see them, China!" Deedee said, her face wrinkled in disgust. "They look like sharks out for the kill. They cruise through the girls, talking to each other about which ones are the cutest. They make bets on which ones they can scam and win."

"They aren't all that way," Mrs. Kiersey had interjected.

"No, they aren't. There's a lot of nice guys. But the few ruin it for everyone else."

"This world will never be without people who just want to satisfy their physical longings, girls," Mrs. Kiersey lectured. "I'm just glad you're wise enough to see them."

Maybe that's why China felt so relaxed around B.T. She knew a friendship was in the making. B.T. wasn't out to scam her or anyone else.

Since B.T. had offered to help again, China gave him the task that would keep him closest to her. "I'll rinse the dishes, and I'll let you run the dishwasher."

"This box is the dishwasher?" B.T. asked, incredulous. "It looks like a breadbox for a giant."

"It's very simple. You slide in one tray at a time through the door on the left. When you close the door tight, the dishwasher goes on. In two minutes, the whole cycle is done. The temperature is so high, it kills any bacteria on the spot."

B.T. stuck his head in the box. "It looks like a car wash for dishes in here. Spigots and whirligigs all over the place."

"Yeah, the water blasts the junk off." China took him to the other side of the washer. "When they're done, you open the right door and slide the tray out. Let them sit in the air for a few minutes. They dry pretty fast. Here, you'll need rubber gloves so you don't scald your hands."

B.T. reached his hand out, gingerly pinching the edge of the gloves. "EEWW! I hate these things. They were always so creepy to me. Ever since I was a little kid, they've bugged me."

"Oh, put them on!" China said in laughing exasperation. "They won't kill you."

"Oh, they won't?" B.T. snapped the gloves on his hands. He stopped, his hands rotating slowly in front of him. "Wow!" he said in mock amazement. "You were right." Without warning, his hands sprang to life, each going in a wildly different direction. B.T. pretended to be yanked about. "Help!" he said in a raspy voice. "They're going to get me. I'll be dead by morning."

One hand zoomed through the dishwasher, emerging out the other side. "Okay, little lady," the gloved hand was obviously saying. "Put down that sprayer or your friend gets it."

China obediently let go of the sprayer. It swung back and forth.

While China had been paying attention to the gloved hand, B.T. had somehow degloved his other hand. He held a towel and started beating the gloved hand with it.

"Back, China!" he shouted. "I'll save us both. Have courage!"

"Stop!" China shrieked, "Stop or I'll die! This stitch in my side is killing me."

"Well, stop laughing then." B.T. wagged his head.

"Females. They blame you for everything." He went to work, acting as if nothing unusual had happened.

China didn't know how to react. She stood, her mouth flapping in the breeze. "How do you do that?" she stammered.

"Do what?" B.T. asked, calmly getting himself into a rhythm with the dish trays and washer.

China figured it best to leave it alone. She finished rinsing the dishes, laughing every time she saw the yellow gloves.

CHAPTER ELEVEN

THEY WALKED TOGETHER TO THE MEETING, B.T. carrying a mysterious paper bag. She asked what he had in there. He opened it and peered inside. The bag jumped as he thumped the bottom and closed it rapidly. "Oh, I'm sorry, my dear girl." Now he sounded like the guy with the buggy eyes in an old black-and-white movie—*The Maltese Falcon.* "This bag is very dangerous. I don't think you should know what's inside. It might hurt you."

Occasionally, China noticed the stares from other campers as they walked. Some of the girls looked intently at China, as if to try to figure out what she had that they didn't. It gave China an uncomfortable feeling. At the same time, she felt kind of proud. Like she might be just a little bit important.

B.T. looked around. "Is Deedee coming?"

China shook her head. "She wanted to hear you sing again, but she didn't really want to sit through the whole meeting. She said she could only stomach it every other night. She hoped you wouldn't mind."

His face fell briefly. Then he exaggerated the look. "Oh, I'm so, so, so sad! I can hardly bear it." He withdrew a make-believe handkerchief and started to weep into it. He turned his head and pretended to blow his nose, all sorts of nasty noises coming from him. Kids in front of him scattered, afraid they might be attacked by this lunatic's nasal spray.

They took the usual front-row seats. B.T. made a big deal out of stowing the paper bag underneath his seat. He talked to it, wrestled with it, and caressed it—all out of China's sight. After that production, B.T. sat like a choirboy, with his hands folded and total attention toward the front. Each time China tried to talk to him, he held his finger to his lips and shook his head. All with a perfectly angelic look on his face.

After the fun songs, Kemper presented his newest revenge—"Tubular Larva Blow." He called up one team member from each insect group. Two at a time, he placed them underneath a see-through contraption. Each person's head could be seen through a lucite box. Into each box was cut a hole, and a plastic tube draped from one hole to the other. In the middle of the tube were six raw eggs without their shells.

"When the whistle sounds, each of you will blow as hard as you can. The winner is the one who doesn't wind up with egg in his mouth." The whistle blew and the eggs seemed to shimmy, shudder, and shake. Then, one unfortunate kid must have had to take a breath.

One moment he seemed fine, the next, raw egg was spilling out of his mouth on to the plastic tarp.

The whole crowd moaned. "Oh, SICK!" cried the girl behind B.T. and China. Even B.T. held his stomach and moaned. "That is so gross."

China nodded. "Kemper is really sick."

Then it was B.T.'s turn to go on stage. His feet came out from underneath his chair. But only one foot had on the tennis shoe he had started out with. The other was a slipper. But not just any slipper.

B.T. limped with exaggerated effort on to the stage. The kids went nuts while B.T. pretended nothing out of the ordinary was happening. Then again, for him, perhaps it wasn't. He moved to the stool and with great effort sat himself upon it. He picked up his guitar and started to strum and pick a little tune. His head bobbed to the rhythm, his slippered foot dangling and twitching in time with his head. The crowd continued to hoot and holler. Then one loud voice screamed, "HEY, B.T.! WHAT'S WITH BERT?"

B.T. looked up from his guitar, startled by the interruption. His eyes scanned the crowd. "What?" he asked in a terribly sweet and innocent voice.

"YOUR SLIPPER!" some girl shouted.

B.T. cupped his hand behind his ear. "I'm sorry. I can't understand you."

The whole crowd screamed almost as one. "Your slipper!"

Looking down at his foot, B.T. seemed startled again. "Well! Would you look at that!" He looked at the crowd, moving his slippered foot so everyone could see. He also admired it himself. "Bert wanted to come to the meeting tonight. He said my toe was looking pretty nasty. So I let him."

Everyone clapped.

"But I had to leave Ernie behind. He left his part of the cabin a total mess. And I told him he was grounded until his room was perfectly clean. Ernie hates phone restriction most of all. So I brought the phone with me, too." He reached into his coat pocket and pulled out a small plastic phone.

China wanted to laugh, but her heart was so full of satisfaction, there was no room for laughter. Instead, she smiled and basked in the warmth of knowing someone so incredible, it was like lying on the beach while the sun made you cozy and drowsy.

After the meeting, Deedee waited for them outside. Her grin told China everything she needed to know.

"Let's go have a chocolate chip shake," Deedee said. "I'm buying!"

At the clubhouse, with one shake between them, B.T. shoveled mounds of thick ice cream into his mouth. "Wow, Deedee!" he teased. "One whole shake to share!"

"I know," Deedee grumbled. "I thought I had more money on me."

After six forbidden autographs and the crowd at the

table growing larger, B.T. excused himself to get to bed.

The moment he was out of earshot, China turned to Deedee. "Well?"

Deedee looked around at the dispersing group, waiting until they had all left. "I felt so awful. So embarrassed. Like I had no business being in his cabin," Deedee started. "But then I remembered—hey, this is B.T! He's crazy. He won't be offended. He keeps things in a total disaster area. I don't know how he finds anything."

"So how did you find them?"

"I figured the one thing most people do is put their underwear in a drawer. So I looked there first. Lo and behold, a nice, neat, brand-new stack right there."

China covered her mouth, wishing she could pull the shades on her imaginative brain that saw them sitting there.

"I bet his mom bought him a whole bunch of new underwear so he wouldn't be embarrassed if he was in a cabin with other guys at camp."

"You'd think having new ones would be more embarrassing."

Deedee nodded. "Anyway, I dumped them in the plastic bag and ran all the way home. It only took about ten minutes to sew them all up."

"Did you sew all the openings shut?"

"Just the legs."

"Do you think he will say anything?"

"Of course," Deedee replied. "He's going to give us a hard time about it."

China's mind went through a bunch of possible scenarios about how he would tell them. Or what he would do. She really wished she could peek in his window and see how he reacted. All the thoughts about his reactions led to other thoughts about this odd thing that was happening whenever she was around B.T. She thought about all the ways he looked at her and talked to her, and she wondered if he was just being nice or if he liked her as a friend, too.

China would never have known she operated in a trance if Deedee hadn't told her.

"What's with you these days?" Deedee asked when they got back to the Kiersey house. "I swear you're in love with B.T. You can't even deny it. It's written all over your face. All over your walk. All over everything you say."

China sat on the edge of the bed and pulled off her shoes, socks, and shirt. The clean, warm sleeping T-shirt fell over her head. She wiggled out of her shorts. Then she flipped her head over and started to brush all her hair into one ponytail at the top of her head. She misted her hair with water and separated it into four portions, rolling each with a clean sock and tying it in a knot.

"See?" Deedee said. "You're even trying to curl your hair. You never curl your hair."

Wrapping her arms around the log that made up one of the posters of Deedee's bed, China rested her chin on top of it. "It's not like that at all."

Deedee held her hairbrush and tapped it in the palm of her hand. "Explain."

"I can't."

"Try."

"You get ready for bed. I'll brush my teeth and think about it."

Observing her odd appearance in the mirror, China slowly brushed her teeth and tried to figure out what this mixture of peace, happiness, and pain was that had taken up residence inside her.

She wondered if anyone else besides Deedee could see what was going on inside. She figured they could. Her fawn-colored eyes had never been known to hide things very well. Most people's eyes told stories no other part of their bodies could. The eyes showed the true feelings of the soul.

How could she describe this whole thing to Deedee? Knowing how most people think, including Deedee, they would totally misread it. Misunderstand it. They would see the deep love that grew like a flower filmed at slow speed, blossoming right before one's eyes at an unbelievable rate. They would say she had a crush. Or that she was in love with him. And she guessed maybe she was. In the strangest sort of way. It wasn't like the time she got a mad crush on her algebra teacher. Or like the new MK who breezed through the language school and was gone in six months. He was her first love. Her first boyfriend. How she felt about B.T. couldn't be compared with how she'd felt about the MK—or ever felt around anybody at all. Especially a guy.

Except . . . wait. That was it! Around B.T., she felt the same safe and whole feeling she did when she was three, eating cinnamon toast at her grandmother Petey's house. Grandma Petey used real butter. And sprinkled the sugar on first, then the cinnamon. They'd sit and talk. Grandma Petey drinking black currant tea, and she, hot apple cider. And then when she was seven. And then again at eleven. Something about that ritual and Grandma Petey gave her a sense of completeness. Even though everything was wrong with the world, there was a safe, warm, and happy place to be.

But could anyone believe you could love a guy so much and still be just friends? Could anyone believe connections like this were possible?

She'd heard of "instant chemistry," but that seemed strictly "hormonal," as her mom would say. That's love at first sight. You don't even have to talk to someone you have chemistry with. All common sense goes out the window and you'd do anything to be by their side. She'd seen enough movies about falling in love to know what the filmmakers said about that.

But this was different. Maybe the fact that both of them were from different cultures made them connect.

Maybe it was something else. Whatever it was, she couldn't figure it out.

Her head popped up, her foamy toothpaste mouth looking like a rabid dog. *Whatever it is, something unusual has happened, and it's like we've been best friends all our lives.*

After rinsing her mouth, she closed the toilet seat and sat, putting her head down on the sink. The cold tile chilled her to goose bumps. If this was such an instant friendship, why did it hurt so much? Why did the pain have to feel like it went right through her heart? *Because,* she thought, *there's no way he could feel the same connection. I'm nuts to ever think he could.*

CHAPTER TWELVE

I've got it all set," B.T. told the girls the next morning. "It took a lot of work. But it's arranged."

China and Deedee looked at each other. Did their practical joke backfire? Why didn't he say anything about it? Maybe he didn't know. Did this say something about B.T.'s personal hygiene they had never anticipated?

"What's arranged?" Deedee's green eyes looked so sparkly from unshed laughter that China had to turn away or she'd bust up laughing first.

"I'm taking you to dinner tonight. At the Forest Ridge Inn."

The potential for laughter fled. Deedee's eyes widened. "You're kidding!"

"Am I supposed to be impressed?" China asked, looking at Deedee's open mouth and wide eyes.

Grabbing China's hands, Deedee looked right into her eyes. "It's only the most elegant place around. People come from all over the valley to eat at this restaurant. It's so posh. Daddy only took us there once." She spun to

111

look at B.T. "Are you aware of how expensive it is?"

"I thought you were going to pay," he innocently replied.

Her mouth gaped. "I, uh . . . " She cleared her throat.

"Of course I know! I wanted to take you guys somewhere nice. To thank you for being such good friends."

Knowing what they had done to him, they both blushed.

Looking to the sky, he said, "Is the sun suddenly hotter? You two have an instant sunburn. It's the oddest thing." He stepped between them and slipped his arms through theirs. "Magda's coming, too. I was able to finagle a night off for her."

"And my mother wouldn't let us go without a chaperon," Deedee said, tossing her head.

B.T. sighed. "So true. But that's okay. I adore Maggie to death. She reminds me of my grandmother."

They moved forward, hindered by B.T.'s odd, stiff gait.

China looked at his slippered foot. Bert had become incredibly dirty. "Is your toe hurting you?"

"Why?"

"You're walking funny."

"It's not my toe."

"What is it, then?"

He looked at her. "It's kind of private."

China swallowed hard. She didn't dare look at Deedee.

He continued. "It's the oddest thing. But certain parts of my clothes simply didn't go on the way they usually do."

Deedee sputtered. China couldn't hold back anymore. All three of them howled with laughter.

Right before they parted ways, B.T. told them, "We have to eat early in order to be back in time for the evening meeting. Be ready by four . . . and don't eat too much lunch."

China didn't pay attention to one thing that happened all that day. Her mind was on what she would wear, because she had nothing suitable for a fancy restaurant. She thought how wonderful it would be to spend the early part of the evening without adoring fans drooling down their backs.

Magda put her to work over the lunch shift and early afternoon, switching her hours with another girl. At 3:30 she and Deedee were throwing clothes out of the drawers and the closet on to the bed. Deedee finally settled for a flowered, cotton dress. The dainty flowers on a cream background, combined with her curly red hair pinned up on one side, made her look very Victorian. For Deedee, there could be no more elegant look.

China felt more at home in baggy things, so she borrowed a white blouse with pearl buttons from Mrs. Kiersey. It looked a little old for her, but it was better than anything else they could find. She wore it with a short scrunch skirt of autumn colors. Neither girl believed in owning nice flats. So they had to borrow these from Mrs. Kiersey also. They felt like Cinderella's stepsisters—China's feet were too small and she had to stuff the toes with toilet paper. Deedee's were too big and she vowed to wear them only when she was walking from the car to the restaurant.

But they had to wear them through the camp, shuffling and muttering about the pinched toes or the sliding feet. They forgot all about their feet when they saw Magda. She looked classy and quite unlike a camp cook in her bold lavender and cream outfit. The girls kept quiet while she struggled to hoist herself up on to the Bronco's front seat. B.T. came to her rescue, standing with his hand still and firm, the gentleman helping the lady on to the coach. He then opened the doors for the girls, helping them up the one giant step.

Magda muttered and fussed the whole way to the inn. "I've never—in all my born days—been to the Forest Ridge Inn. And I can't believe I'm going right now."

The fragrant forest blew its perfume into the open windows, filling the car with pine-scented ambrosia. Leaning her head back on the seat, China couldn't decide whether to wear her sunglasses or not. One moment sunshine blinded her. The next, interlaced trees created dark shadows and she had to take off her sunglasses to enjoy it all. The temperature changed with the appearance and disappearance of the sun. In the shade, she was cool, her skin covered with goose bumps. In the sun, she felt warm.

Nothing could compare with the beauty of the majestic mountains—their craggy peaks so high above her, the zillions of trees and zillions of colors. No smell could cleanse her all the way to her soul like the smell of fresh pine. And dirt. *How can you explain the smell of dirt?* she wondered. *Or of a creek?* But there are different smells for those things. Even the dust that clung to the inside of her nostrils had its own fragrance. Warm. Earthy.

Deedee bounced in her seat. "There it is!" she said, pointing up the side of the mountain. China strained to distinguish the log building from the masses of trees surrounding it. The building seemed to hang on the cliff. A shiver zipped through China. She didn't much like the thought of being in a building like that if an earthquake hit. It seemed to barely touch the mountainside, depending on stilts to hold it up. Sunlight on glass was the only way to tell a building was there. And there was plenty of glass. Aside from the necessary casings, it seemed to be all glass. Huge paned windows.

It took five more minutes of winding mountain road before they reached the inn. The main restaurant looked quite plain from the road. No windows on that side. A heavy door made of pine logs had a twisted curve of wrought iron for the handle. A wisp of smoke curled up into the trees, getting caught in the branches before separating. Feeling awkward, China stepped from the car and stood, her hands wishing they had a purse or jacket or something else to hold on to. Across the road, buried in the trees, she could make out little bits of red tile and green shingle. Sprinkled about, these were the cabins that made up the "inn" part of the Forest Ridge complex.

B.T. held out his arm to Magda. "Shall we?" he said in the most grown-up, polite tone China ever heard coming out of the mouth of a seventeen-year-old guy. Magda rewarded his efforts with another one of her soft, approving mother looks.

At the door, he let go of Magda. He pulled the heavy door open and held it there while they, feeling quite a bit like royal ladies, walked into the dark, comforting room. Most of the furnishings were made from things found on the mountain—polished dark wood floors, stone lower walls changing to wood at about tabletop level. Persian rugs of red, black, and royal blue lay on the floors. A bench in the waiting area had once been a large tree, now with a wedge cut out of it so they could sit comfortably on cushions of tapestry.

China could smell the elegance, sense it in the mannerisms of the workers. They almost seemed to glide when they moved. No sharp, glaring movements. When they spoke, their voices were calm and soft.

The maitre d' looked completely at home in his dark

suit and white gloves. He approached them, the sun-light of the afternoon making B.T. a silhouette in the doorway.

"May I help you, ladies?" he asked, quite reserved and unimpressed. China wondered if anything ever fazed this man. *Traffic? Waiting in long lines? Probably not.* She couldn't imagine him hang gliding. Or going off the Blob. She swallowed her smile and tried to be the sophisticated person she was supposed to be.

As the door closed, B.T. moved to the front of the little group. China's eyes attempted to adjust to the dark room.

"We'd like a table for four. With a nice view," B.T. said authoritatively, as if he were used to having people obey his commands.

China wanted to laugh. *Oh, come on, B.T. You're just a KID. Who's going to listen to you?*

The maitre d' began to say something, but then his eyes widened, his eyebrows moved in a wiggly sort of way, and he bowed low at the waist. "If you don't mind, sir, I would like to prepare a special table for you myself."

"I'm sure it will be worth the wait," B.T. said graciously.

Deedee turned to China, raising her eyebrows in a look that said, *Hmm! This is interesting.*

A few moments later, the maitre d' returned and bowed again. "Right this way, sir."

As they passed tables with early diners, the conversations seemed to stop for a moment, then change pace and tone to rapid whispers. And then silence again. China felt many pairs of eyes boring into her back. Something changed in the room. It went from a quiet, somber mood to one full of expectation and excitement.

China always thought a place to eat really couldn't be something special. But somehow this was beyond anything she'd ever dreamed. It could only be described as magnificent. And the table where the maitre d' seated them could be nothing less than incredible. China tried to take it all in without looking completely in awe at the richness in front of her. An ivory linen tablecloth looked more like silk than linen. Real sterling silver place settings. Stemmed crystal drinking glasses. Six perfect white rosebuds in an ornate silver vase. Forest green napkins of the same linen as the tablecloth were folded as upright fans at each place. Never had China been to a place that proudly displayed such elegance. Such class. Such wealth. The beauty seemed to transform something inside her, and she wanted to move with poise and elegance like those around her. Instead, she felt like an old horse stumbling over pebbles.

The maitre d' seated each of the girls, pulling their chairs from the table, then laying their napkins in their laps. B.T. did the same for Magda.

"Pierre will be here to serve you this evening," the maitre d' said.

China had to run her fingers lightly over the tablecloth to see if it felt as silky soft as it looked. "My grandmother had cloths like these," Magda muttered, her fingers also moving across it. "But she only used them at Christmas and Easter. She covered them with clear plastic so we could see but not touch. I used to sneak my fingers underneath the plastic to feel it."

"Where are the menus?" Deedee asked, looking around.

"They'll come," B.T. said. "A place like this doesn't want you to rush. They want you to enjoy being pampered."

Pierre came and poured them all mineral water and presented an hors d'oevre China couldn't pronounce. "Compliments of the chef," he said with a smile and a bow.

"Look at that," Magda said in the soft voice she'd been using ever since they'd boarded the Bronco for their trip to the inn.

China turned to look at the view and almost gasped aloud. As far as she could see, there were trees and mountains and crags and valleys and granite cliffs and scars from old landslides. Way off in the distance, smog covered the valley like a dirty brown blanket. Off to the right, she thought she could make out some of the buildings of Camp Crazy Bear. It seemed they hung in the air and had become the top of an old pine tree.

It also seemed they had been given the best table. Others had to peer through tall trees to see the view. They had the only unobstructed view. "Oh, zareba!" she exhaled.

B.T. laughed. "Zareba?"

"I borrowed it from you. It's the only word I can say at a time like this."

Deedee leaned across China and looked down, backing up quickly. "I'm glad you're sitting there and not me." She shivered. "It makes me more woozy than a merry-go-round."

Following B.T.'s lead, China helped herself to the hors d'oeuvre. She smeared some black stuff over a thick cracker bread. It tasted salty and dark. Rich and ugly. Maybe something from the sea. She wasn't sure if she liked it or not and was glad B.T. didn't encourage her to have more.

The hors d'oeuvre disappeared slowly. Magda, if she talked at all, talked in soft, awed tones. China couldn't take her eyes off the view—as long as she didn't look down, she was okay. Deedee watched the hovering employees without saying anything. B.T. gave directions in quiet, authoritative words.

The menus arrived after the hors d'oevre had been whisked away. Opening the leather cover, China felt her eyes bulge. She couldn't believe the prices. One silly plate of food cost more than her parents would spend taking the whole family to a Guatemalan-style junk food place. Most of the food was stuff she'd never heard of before. She couldn't even pronounce half of their names.

Uncomfortable silence hung over the table. China elbowed Deedee. She held her menu up in front of her face so that B.T. and Magda couldn't see her. "What are we supposed to order?" she mouthed to Deedee.

Deedee, looking as wide-eyed and confused as China, shrugged her shoulders in response.

B.T. closed his menu and laid it on the table in front of him. "I'm always a sucker for swordfish. Done right, there's nothing better in the world."

China found the swordfish. The second most expensive thing on the menu. She sighed. "I guess I'll try that, too."

Deedee shook her head. "I'll have the steak thing. I don't like fish much."

Closing her menu, Magda tucked a wisp of hair back into place. "I haven't had rack of lamb in years. I'll take that."

The real shock came when China realized the meal didn't come with soup, salad, potato, or anything else. Those things all had to be chosen separately. Also with huge price tags attached.

The awkward silence continued after Pierre had taken their requests back to the kitchen.

Pierre returned almost immediately, looking awkward and flustered. He wrung his hands and stood on one foot and then the other. "I'm sorry, sir," he stammered, "but I have a rather uncomfortable request to make."

"Yes, Pierre?" B.T. said, looking him right in the eyes.

"Our chef, he, well, he has asked me to ask you . . . "

All eyes watched him, waiting for him to spit out what he wanted.

" . . . he wishes that I secure an autograph from . . . "

B.T. smiled broadly. "Sure! Of course! Why didn't you say so? I had no idea the fame of our own cook, Magda, had reached so far and wide. I'm sure she wouldn't mind giving her autograph."

The girls held their laughter in check as B.T. spoke, but the minute they saw the confused and then unflappable person disintegrate in front of them, they could hold it back no longer. Magda started the whole thing with a rumble the girls knew as her laughter gathering itself to pour out. At poor Pierre's expense, they laughed and laughed, quite unbecoming to people who were supposed to behave in an elegant establishment.

CHAPTER THIRTEEN

THE LAUGH WAS ALL THEY NEEDED TO BREAK the ice. They weren't elegant people playing elegant games in an elegant restaurant. They were good friends enjoying a fabulous meal in a fabulous place. They could be themselves and enjoy the incredible, probably once-in-a-life-time experience.

Throughout the meal they told stories, laughing at some, booing at others. Never far away, Pierre hovered, waiting for the moment a fork rested on an empty plate, the final piece of San Francisco sourdough bread was lifted from the basket, the last of the butter spread. Without asking, their every need was filled.

After the final dinner plate had been removed, a silver-handled whisk brush swept crumbs into a minia-ture silver dustbin. Smooth, creamy lemon mousse arrived with coffee. Pierre placed a truffle tree in the middle of the table. And too soon, dinner, dessert, and the special time was over.

Looking at his watch, B.T. made the sad announce-ment. "Ladies, we need to get back." Reaching for

Magda's and Deedee's hands, he squeezed them tight. He looked into everyone's eyes, holding China's the longest. "I wanted you guys to know how much I appreciate you." He looked down for a moment, as if gathering his thoughts. Then he looked mostly from China to Deedee. "I also wanted you guys to know what it's like to live in my world. To really understand me and be my friend, you need to see these things so you can decide where you want to go with it. It's not easy."

China wanted to ask B.T. what he meant, but as she opened her mouth to ask, a very excited, breathless girl about their age approached them. "May I please have my picture taken with you?" she gushed all over B.T. as he stood from the table, helping Magda and then Deedee from their chairs.

B.T. helped China, then draped his arm around her. "Honey," he droned, "would you mind so terribly if I had my picture taken with this young lady?"

China put on an exaggerated pout. "Oh, sweetheart! You know how I hate these things." She paused while B.T. looked at her so expectantly. She almost but not quite lost her character. "Oh, all right! Just this once."

The girl handed her camera to Magda and gave quick instructions. Her face was bright red and she tried to contain her excitement at being so close to someone famous.

As soon as the camera clicked, B.T. signed his autograph on the back of a blank bill. "Follow God!" he said brightly to her, and she looked bewildered.

He put his arm around China and guided her out the door, saying, "Now, that wasn't so bad, was it?"

China could feel the girl's jealousy following them all the way out the door.

In the car, Deedee wore a look of deep contemplation while Magda and B.T. laughed and talked in the front seat. China poked Deedee. "Now it's your turn to be lost in another world. What's going on?"

Deedee shook her head. She looked at B.T. and then back at China with a warning look. "Tonight. In bed. I'll tell you then."

"Hey!" B.T. called. "What're you two up to back there? Not planning anymore jokes, are you?"

"Are you kidding?" Deedee asked. "After all that? We'd be the jerks of the century to do anything mean to you."

"You'd better not ever use anything as an excuse to not play jokes on me," B.T. warned. He sounded almost hurt. "Or I won't ever be nice to you again."

"Does that always happen?" Deedee asked. "You know, what the maitre d' did at the end."

B.T. frowned and nodded. "All the time." He didn't elaborate, and neither did Deedee. China hoped she would fill her in later.

Returning to camp and the evening meeting was such a letdown. Being treated like royalty seemed to have changed something inside China. All at once the old buildings and cabins seemed shabby. All she had loved and cared about and enjoyed looked boring. And plain. And almost repulsive. The kids so childish. The games even more so. Both girls left the meeting after B.T. played.

Walking through the dusk, they absently swatted mosquitoes. Deedee took off her tight shoes and carried them in her hand. China slipped hers off, too.

"Did you notice there were no disasters? The restaurant didn't fall into the canyon. No one spilled boiling coffee on B.T. It was like he was a different person."

China laughed. "Maybe when he's Mr. Television Star, he's not accident-prone."

Deedee looked distant, thoughtful. "There was something really odd though . . . "

China turned to walk to the shore of Little Bear Lake. She smoothed her skirt and sat on the sand with her shoes next to her. Little Bear smelled cool and a little musty.

Deedee dropped next to her. "I told you Dad took us there before."

"Yeah. I can't believe how much it cost!"

"I can tell you it's far more elegant now than when we went there. But there's something else bothering me. Some of the people were the same as when Dad took us. But they didn't treat us that nice. They waited on us and were polite and all. But they didn't look like vultures waiting for us to finish every little thing. They didn't treat us like we were the president. Or royalty."

"Or like television stars," China added.

"Yeah."

"But maybe that's their new policy—to go along with the higher prices."

Deedee took the clip out of her hair and shook it free. She dug her fingers into the roots and lifted up, fluffing her hair out. "I don't think so. No one else in that restaurant had that kind of service. I watched."

China considered what Deedee said. Soaked it all in. She looked out across Little Bear's surface, ruffled by the evening breeze.

"Did you hear what the maitre d' said?" Deedee continued.

"What?"

"He didn't charge B.T. for his meal. Just ours."

China looked back at her, confused. "Why would he do that?"

"He told B.T. it was because it was such a pleasure to serve him. So nice that B.T. chose his restaurant to grace his presence with."

China rolled her eyes. "That's stupid."

"I don't think it's fair either. My dad works so hard and can hardly afford to take his wife out to dinner, much less his five kids. He doesn't get any breaks when he goes anywhere. Why do people give movie stars a break but not regular people?"

"Is that what you asked B.T. about in the car?"

"Yeah. It makes me mad."

China stuck her legs out in front of her, crossing her ankles. She put her hands behind her so she could look up at the emerging stars. "What do you think it would be like to live like that all the time?"

Digging her toes into the sand, Deedee was quiet. Her chin rested on her knees as she gazed across the surface of the lake. "I don't know if I'd like that."

"Come on! You wouldn't like to be treated like that all the time? All those people being so nice to you?" China's heart beat faster at the thought.

"Yeah. I guess I could get used to that."

Both girls were quiet for a moment. China said softly, "Maybe that's why Heather was the way she was. It's rather nice having people hang on every word you say as if it were the funniest or wisest or most important thing ever said."

"Why isn't everything we say important—even if we aren't somebody famous?" Deedee's fingers disappeared into the sand.

"Maybe because we all talk too much."

Kemper's voice rose and fell. The sound carried all the way from Sweet Pea Lodge, but the words got lost somewhere along the way.

"I heard some of the kids talking," Deedee told her. "They said B.T. is so rich, if he quit working today, he'd have enough money to last the rest of his entire life. He's a multimillionaire!"

China's mind reeled at the thought. *Not work? Not*

have to work? Her words eased from her as if they were a sigh. "What would it be like to not only be rich, but to also be well known? I'd never really thought about it before. It was all so impossible." She shook her head. "Look at B.T.! He's rich and famous."

"I could travel," Deedee said suddenly, her voice brighter.

"What are you talking about?"

"If I had someone famous as my boyfriend or best friend, I could travel. I could go to Greece."

China jumped into the game, her mind already spending big bucks. "If I were rich, I could travel first class. And the flight attendants wouldn't look at me like I was interrupting something when I asked for a pillow or for decent food."

"I could go to Hawaii every year."

"Or the States every summer."

"And if we were famous," Deedee said, her voice in awe, "you know people would run home and tell everyone that they saw you and talked with you."

"Or that bigwig so and so was seen with a gorgeous girl."

Deedee pretended to poof up her hair.

"You could buy anything."

"Clothes. Lots and lots of clothes," Deedee said.

"And you wouldn't have to wait for a sale!" China thought aloud in amazement. Never in her life had she been able to buy something brand new, off the rack.

Most of her stuff came from missionary barrels. Anything bought had to be off the clearance rack.

"I could get my clothes and shoes tailor-made."

"We wouldn't have to borrow shoes that were too big or too little," China said, laughing.

"I could buy my mom some nice furniture."

"Mmmm," China thought out loud. "I could buy a camp."

"A house. You could buy a house."

"With a great big television."

"With all the channels," Deedee added.

"I bet you could be taken to the front of the line at Disneyland."

"And Six Flags. "

"We could eat out at every meal," China said.

"Go to every movie."

"Especially the ones we starred in."

"When we'd go to the Academy Awards in a limousine, all these people would be screaming because they can't believe they're seeing us in person," Deedee said.

"Or if you aren't famous enough, you could still go on HIS arm. You'd still be held in awe and appreciation, and everyone would be jealous of you and wonder who you were and how in the world you got so lucky to be there."

"We could go anywhere and get special service," Deedee said.

"No matter what, people would be real friendly and

nice wherever you went. They would want to be nice because they'd hope maybe you would give them five minutes of your time." China breathed on her nails with a haughty air and buffed them on her shirt.

They sat in silence, breathing in the joyful dreams of what they could be. What nice things could happen. How the world would be a better place if they too had status like B.T. *People would look up to me. And respect me. No one would be mean to me again,* China thought.

"My mind is working overtime again," China said after a long silence.

"Uh-oh. That means trouble."

She sighed. "I know."

"What's it brewing this time?" Deedee asked.

"Did B.T. mean what he said? Did he say we had to make a decision about how far we wanted to go with this?"

"Yeah," Deedee said hesitantly.

"I wonder if . . . if what he meant was . . . well . . . I know it sounds crazy, but . . . "

"What?"

"Maybe he could get us on the TV show. Maybe a bit part or something."

Deedee's wiggling fingers and toes stopped their burrowing. "I hadn't thought of that. Do you know how many people get their start that way?"

The lake and stars and moon disappeared from view.

The girls could no longer see or hear what went on around them. What went on inside their imaginations had grown so strong, it blocked out everything else. And the daydreams became as real as the lake and the sand had been just moments before.

CHAPTER FOURTEEN

CHINA COULDN'T SLEEP. THOUSANDS OF thoughts dressed in audience applause and fabulous clothes and delicious gourmet meals kept going through her head. The more she thought about it, the more she hungered for it. Wanted it. Believed it could be her purpose in life. Maybe that's why God had brought her to Camp Crazy Bear. Maybe it was to meet B.T.—get to be friends—and then get a small part in his show. And then someone would see her and put her in a series or an academy award–winning film. She could tell everyone about God. *That's It! I could be a missionary to Hollywood! I know all about being a missionary. And like B.T. said, it's just another culture of unsaved people needing to be told about God. And when I make lots of money, I can buy a camp and send kids there.*

China curled up inside her sleeping bag. She scrunched her pillow into a softer poof.

Wow, God! she prayed. *You're incredible. So amazing in how you do stuff! Mom always said you had great plans and weird ways you work things out.*

She bolted upright in bed. "Mom!"

"Uh?" came a muffled grunt from the bed next to her.

"I haven't written Mom in ages!" China whispered. She dropped back to her pillow. "Come to think of it, she hasn't written me either."

"Nff nrt fis nis nuf," Deedee mumbled. Her breathing fell into a low, heavy pattern.

China scrounged quietly around the room until she found pen, paper, and a small flashlight.

Dear Mom,

You'll never believe what's happening. I'll have to tell you later when everything is more settled. But I think I know why God wanted me to come here. I've met this really fab guy. He's not a boyfriend or anything, but he's really cool. And I think God put him here, and me here, so we could meet and then some neat stuff could happen. You are right. God sometimes does things in a real roundabout way. Would you mind if I lived with Aunt Liddy after the summer, if things work out?

Work is going fine. I hope you're all fine. I know I'm supposed to miss you. Sorry I don't. I don't mean that as being nasty. I'm just having a great time here, so there isn't time to miss you.

In the bedroom after breakfast the next morning, Deedee tied her hiking boot and let her foot slam on the floor. She put the other foot on the side of the bed to lace and tie the other shoe. "So. What'll we do this morning?"

"Let's go watch the competition."

Deedee shook her head. "I'd rather go horseback riding. Or take a hike. We haven't been on a hike in a long time. I'm tired of the kids. We don't know anyone anyway."

"What about B.T.?"

"I can live without B.T. this morning," Deedee said in an acid tone. "Can't you?"

China looked at her, confused. "I thought you liked B.T."

"I did. I mean, I do." Deedee sighed and let her other foot fall to the floor. "Look. We had some fun dreaming last night. But that's all it was. Dreaming. It ain't never gonna happen, girlfriend."

"You never know. God opens crazy doors."

"Not in this neck of the woods."

"So what does that have to do with B.T.?"

"I don't know if I trust him. I'm tired of seeing him change so much. One minute he's a cowboy. The next he's Popeye. The next he's a rich kid treating the poor folk to a fancy dinner. The next he's someone else. Instead of two-faced, B.T. is about 100-faced. How do you know who's the real B.T.?"

"I know," China said with confidence.

"Yeah, right." Deedee took a pick and tried to run it

through her thick curls. "Is he trying to buy us off with an expensive dinner? What is he? Some kind of rich show-off?"

"NO! I got to know him real well night before last. He really opened up while we worked in the kitchen." China sat on the edge of the bed and braided her hair into a french braid. "He's not like what you said. He's real thoughtful. A strong Christian. He really cares about people."

"And you believe that's the real B.T.? How do you know it isn't just one of his many acts? One of his many costumes. Come on, China! The guy can become who-ever he wants whenever he wants. His taking us out to dinner was an awfully fancy show to put on for us. What does he want from us? I think we're going along like two little dummies ready to let him be our ventriloquist."

China's mouth dropped open. "I don't believe you said that. He's a great guy."

"Yeah. He's a lot of fun. But I don't trust him."

"Okay. Don't. But I do. I think God put him here for a reason."

"What? So you can be on television?"

YES! China wanted to scream. Instead, she didn't answer. She tried to keep her face closed and expres-sionless. The girls walked outside, letting the screen door slam.

Deedee's arms flew out. "You really think this outlandish dream we had last night is going to come true, don't you?" Deedee slapped her forehead. "That's all daydreaming, China. It's not going to happen. Not to you, not to me, and probably never to anyone we know."

"God does some weird things, Deedee."

"You've lost your mind, China. B.T. must be some kind of monster to have eaten your mind like that. Enjoy him while he's here. But don't think it's going to last past Saturday. He's going to go back to his world and you'll still be in yours. Poor. Living in ugly clothes that used to belong to someone else. You're not a star, China. And I'll bet you never will be."

"Thanks a lot! You're really a great friend!" China spat the words.

"True friends tell you the truth."

"The truth is, you couldn't be my friend if you don't believe in me. If you don't support me."

"Oh. Am I supposed to support stupidity? Well, you can forget that. I hope I'll never be that sort of friend." Deedee spun and stomped off, her hiking boots making dust clouds behind her.

China dropped on to a rock. She wondered if what Deedee said was right. She tried to fit it in with her newest revelation. And none of it fit.

She got up and began to walk somewhere. She didn't really know where. Without thinking, she followed the shouts and screams the teams of insects on the Battlefield.

A rousing game of pushball moved about the Battlefield. On one end, a strange commotion seemed to be taking place. "Hey ya!" B.T. called, waving at China.

"What are you doing?" China asked, looking around at bodies strewn about the grass.

B.T. stood behind a tripod, a video camera perched on top. "I got bored. I can't play the good games with this stupid toe. So I thought maybe we should make life a little more exciting for those who aren't playing. We're making a commercial for the camp."

China looked about. Some of the bodies played dead. Others moaned and looked on their way to relief through dying. A few staggered into the picture and collapsed.

"It looks like the bubonic plague."

"Close. It's the Eelapuash plague. Later I'll go film Eelapuash, and everyone eating. This is the result of eating there. Aren't they great actors?"

An electric excitement passed through China, exploding a thought in her brain. *This is it! This is how I can show him what I look like on film. How I can act. Without it being too obvious.*

"Do you want me to do anything, B.T.?"

"No. The kids won't recognize you if you're in the film."

China's heart fell. "I can be the nurse. Or the camp representative."

"Okay. Think of something."

China went to the edge of the writhing, dying crowd and watched for a moment, trying to think fast. *Come on, you stupid brain! When I want you to shutup you spit out zillions of ideas. When I want you to spit out ideas, you're empty. This isn't fair. When are you going to cooperate?*

"China! You're on!"

China gave him a sick grin and walked on to the Battlefield. "Oh, dear! What's happening?" she asked, trying to be dramatic. "All our children are dying!"

"Cut!" B.T. said. He pulled China aside. "Try again. This time be funny. Do something to make people laugh."

China moved off to the side, her brain still not cooperating. When B.T. motioned to her, she skipped out into the group and tripped over one of the bodies. "My! The rocks are getting soft around here!" She picked herself up and continued to skip.

"CUT!" B.T. pulled her aside again. "Fabulous," he said in a Hollywood voice. "Don't call us, we'll call you."

"I did good, huh?" China said, her voice sounding incredibly fake even to herself. "I bet I could be on TV, too." She hated herself for saying it, but on the other hand, she didn't want to miss an important moment.

Something disappeared from B.T.'s face. China couldn't figure out what that was, but it was like the door to a giant, well-lit house had suddenly closed and the lights went out. "You did okay," B.T. said flatly.

The teams on the field switched, and B.T. had the new group weeping for their lost friends. China watched from the sidelines, grinning at B.T. whenever she could. Once in a while, she'd go up and ask if he needed her to do something else. "No, I've got it," he told her every time. When he finished, he folded the tripod legs together and picked up the whole thing as a unit. China went over to him. "Where are you going?"

"Eelapuash."

"Can I go?"

"I guess."

China half walked, half skipped, and in general could not contain all the excited energy bursting through her. "How do people get on your show?" *Shut up, China. I'm telling you to shut up,* her inner voice told her. China ignored it.

B.T. looked at her carefully, then watched the path while he talked. "Through an agent."

"How do you get an agent?" China's palms got sweaty. She knew she shouldn't say another word but couldn't seem to stop herself.

"You have to go on an interview, send pictures . . . . Why are you asking me this?"

China shrugged. "I don't know." Her face flamed with heat, and she let her voice trail off. "Uh, just interested."

They walked a little way more in silence. China began to feel uncomfortable. B.T. was never quiet with her. She had to say something. "Do you ever get your friends on the show?"

B.T.'s head dropped as if he watched every tiny rock on the ground as they passed. "Once in a while."

"How neat!" China said, her voice ending in a little squeak. China wanted to gag herself. Disappear. *Why am I saying such stupid things?*

"Hey, look," B.T. said. "I've changed my mind about filming at Eelapuash right now. I think I'll wait until dinner. The light will be better. I'm going to practice my guitar until lunch." Without turning to say good-bye, he walked away.

China felt her heart sink to the bottom of her shoes.

CHAPTER FIFTEEN

HI, CHINA HONEY," MAGDA CALLED AS China entered the kitchen.

China took a clean folded apron from the stack. Dropping the neck loop over her head, she tied the strings around her waist in front. "Hi, Magda."

China set to work pushing the dish cart into the dining room to set tables. She gave a forced smile to Rick, who tried to pull her into a quick jig around the kitchen. She pushed him gently away. "I'd better work," she said in a quiet voice.

As she walked away, she heard him singing "Just you wait, Henry Higgins." She knew the song from *My Fair Lady*. Eliza had gotten tired of her teacher's attitude toward her. China sighed. *It's too bad if he thinks I have an attitude.*

She liked the clatter of the plastic plates hitting the table. An odd, pleasantly pitched sound. She let them land so they would halfspin for just a moment, making the sound last a little longer.

Today the work seemed different. Today the kitchen

looked strange. Small. Too small. Eelapuash itself looked a little dingy and dull. Almost on the shabby side. Awful colored plastic chairs of outlandish orange and putrid yellow. Folding chairs. Some bent. Some written on with felt pen. All had seen better days.

If I were on a series, I wouldn't have to do this kind of work anymore. She thought. *It's so stupid. And repetitive. Two hundred plates set on twenty round tables. Two hundred glasses. Two hundred knives. Two hundred everything. Three times a day. Washing them three times a day.*

Suddenly, it all seemed so pointless. Eating seemed pointless. Wasting so much time preparing for it, doing it, then cleaning up after it. She knew her attitude stunk, but its hold on her was like a blood-sucking leech.

B.T. burst through the door talking to himself, the video camera perched on his shoulder. He stopped dead when he saw China. "I'm sorry. I thought it would be empty."

"Do you think the tables set themselves by magic?" China wished her words could evaporate. But they seemed to hang there like a cloud of poisonous gas. "I'm sorry," she said immediately.

B.T. looked at her, his eyes searching her face, almost desperate for something. China felt awkward. She decided to derail the whole situation by saying something that was probably more stupid but at least not painful. "Do you ever think about how strange eating is?"

A crooked smile appeared. "What do you mean?"

"At least three times a day, we put stuff in our mouths. If we don't do it, we get crabby, then sick, then die. This stuff we put in our mouths is very important. It is so important that we build huge buildings so others can go find stuff to put in their mouths. We walk up and down long aisles and stare at this stuff and put some of the things in baskets."

B.T. nodded his head, his crooked smile growing bigger. "Rigwiddi."

"And then there are other buildings where we go (some that hang off of mountainsides over canyons) to have someone else make this stuff to put in our mouths. We take people with us to these buildings so we can put this stuff in our mouths together. I tell you, it's so strange!"

"I never really thought about it that way." B.T. chuckled.

Then China noticed the red light on the video camera. "You didn't."

"I did. I never miss a Kodak moment."

"Zarf," China said, then started dropping plates on to the tables once again.

"Here," B.T. said, the camera still rolling, "you can see one of those peerless workers . . . "

"Don't you mean fearless?"

"No. Peerless. Please stop interrupting."

"Sorry."

"A peerless worker preparing to entice these poor young people to their hapless deaths. A new crowd will be pouring in here soon, believing they will be receiving nourishment for their growing adolescent bodies."

China paused from her plate setting and looked up at the camera and shook her head. She resumed the plate clattering.

Maneuvering through the tables, B.T. said, "Over here is the door behind which all the tragedy could be averted." He disappeared into the kitchen.

China went back to her thoughts. Everything inside her jumbled together. The question of B.T. as friend or door opener to her future mingled with the incredible feeling of knowing what money could buy. *See? There is so much that's more important in life than eating. Why does eating have to be so important? Magda wastes her whole life feeding others. What a waste! And this is where I am? Well, not for long.*

Grabbing handfuls of knives, she began placing them around the tables. Her thoughts marched onward, trudging through the mud of her past life. Her life in Guatemala. The mud of trying to get along with her mom. Of trying to avoid her brothers, Cam and Nic, as much as possible. Of wishing her dad were home more often, then wishing he was gone when he was home.

Her thoughts surveyed all the things she didn't like

about life in general. Boring, mostly. Boring and difficult, with a few good days thrown in. Until Camp Crazy
Bear. She loved the camp and her work. Until now. Now
that her future work might be more important than
this, she couldn't wait to get out. Couldn't wait to move
on to the exciting work in Hollywood that God seemed
to want to put her into.

The knives done, she started on the spoons. The
spoons done, she started on the forks. Completing each
table made her feelings grow. Feelings that the whole
tablesetting process was so unnecessary. Meant for
someone who didn't have more important things to do.

Dissatisfaction grew in her heart. One thought
seemed to take root and grow tentacles under the surface where she couldn't see how fast it spread. By the
time the napkins were safely tucked underneath the
forks, China could barely stand to be in Eelapuash.
Bursting through the swinging door into the kitchen,
she almost slammed into Rick.

"Whoa! China!"

"Magda," China called, ignoring Rick. "What now?"

"We had a casserole spill in oven number three. I
think it's cooled down enough to clean it out now."

"Fine," grumbled China.

"You certainly need some pepping up," Rick said.

"Take a hike."

"I will tomorrow morning. With Bologna. Not now,
thanks." Rick adjusted his blue sport cap and limped

into the oven area.

China felt a twinge of guilt. But only a twinge, easily pushed aside and forgotten.

All through the evening, the bright kitchen lost its brightness. It lost its wit and fun. Instead, it grew more and more stupid. More boring. The most wasted time China had ever spent in her life.

God, when are you going to get me out of here? I can't take it anymore she prayed. *Rick's endless songs and dumb jokes. Magda's hillbilly "wisdom" bursting at the seams and wrapped in this sickening sweet kindness. I could gag on it all.*

China skipped the evening meeting, preferring to sit on the sand watching spots of the camp's night lights shimmering on Little Bear Lake. The moon and stars were hidden behind a layer of clouds. She didn't even care that Deedee wasn't there. She didn't even know what Deedee was doing.

The only thing that soothed her frustrating desire to throw herself on to her future was hearing B.T.'s strong voice wafting from Sweet Pea Lodge. She sat up straighter. He was singing an old hymn. With a new twist. "Trust and obey. For there's no other way, to be happy in Jesus, but to trust and obey."

"I'm trying to trust and obey, God. But things aren't happening fast enough." She tossed a small rock into the water.

God didn't answer. He didn't answer very often. At

least not in the ways China wished he would. If he couldn't manage to talk to her, then he could at least send letters or packages. Or maybe an angelic visitor. Or a dream. Or a vision. Not that she'd know the difference between a regular visitor or dream and one from God. Not that she really knew what a vision was either. But she figured she'd know when it happened.

Then came the rise and fall of Kemper's voice. Teaching. Always teaching. Always trying to give the kids something to hold on to in a crazy world. But China didn't need that anymore. Her world wasn't going to be crazy. It finally had purpose and direction.

Someone approached the lake, shoes scrunching in the sand. A big person sat next to her. China turned halfway, then back to the lake. Rick. He didn't say anything. He just sat. Then someone else sat on the other side of her. Deedee.

Kemper stopped talking and the kids started pouring out of the building.

"Just the two people I wanted to see," Rick said abruptly, as if he had just walked up to them on a trail somewhere. "B.T. said he wanted us to go to his cabin for something. I'm not sure what."

"We shouldn't go in his cabin," Deedee said. "It's not right."

"I guess that's why I'm invited."

"But you are also of the male species," Deedee told him.

"I'm glad you noticed. I checked it out with your mom. Not to worry."

Rick leaned over to China and said softly, "I hope you're feeling better now."

China shrugged her shoulders. But inside, the awful feelings and frustration disappeared the minute Rick said B.T. wanted her. New feelings of hope, belonging, and peace flooded her. But she didn't want to look too eager. Didn't want Deedee to think the wrong things. So she said nothing. She didn't move. She waited for someone else to stand first.

Rick seemed to be waiting for something. So China slid back into her thoughts and forgot everything else.

CHAPTER SIXTEEN

After the kids had cleared off the trails, without a word Rick stood and started to walk away. Both girls followed him.

"Did he say what he wanted?" China asked.

"He just said he had a treat for us."

Deedee stopped. "I don't think I can stand another of his treats. It's out of my league. It makes me want things I can't have. That's not fair."

"Oh, I don't think it's much," Rick said casually.

On the other end of the spectrum, China's heart started to beat faster, eagerly expecting a new glimpse into the world of the privileged. She was so lost in her thoughts that she didn't see the trees, the path, Deedee, or Rick in front of her. She only saw what was in her head. It wasn't until Deedee stopped short and gasped that she came out of it. They were off the regular path, taking a shortcut to B.T.'s cabin. The trees grew thick and close, the chaparral nearby but not close enough to hinder their walk.

"What is that?" Deedee whispered, looking off into

the trees.

Rick had stopped a few feet ahead. "What?" he said in a normal voice.

"Shhh." Deedee put her finger to her lips and pointed.

China peered through the darkness. Something moved. She could see it, but not quite.

"Come here," Rick whispered. "I can see real good from here."

The girls crowded around him, standing close behind him.

The thing moved again, floating silently. They could see it, but they couldn't hear it. At first China thought it was hanging from a tree, but then it moved away. There was no way it could be attached. She felt a shiver run up her spine.

Deedee reached over and linked pinkies with China. "What is it?" she asked again.

Rick didn't answer. China *couldn't* answer. They all watched and waited.

The thing moved up and down. Bobbing almost. And then it would stop and move abruptly from side to side. Then it moved in circles.

"Whatever it is, it's the weirdest thing I've ever seen," China whispered.

"It's amazing," Rick said in an exhale.

"Is it coming closer?" Deedee asked, her pinkie tightening its grip.

China stuck her head out as if that would help her see it better. She didn't want to think Deedee was right, but she was.

The thing was pure white and oval. As it came closer, it looked like . . . but it couldn't be. The girls looked at each other and China shivered again. When China looked back, she knew. "It's a face . . . "

"But how could it . . . " Deedee's voice trailed off. China swore she knew what Deedee was thinking. How could a face be floating? Where was the body? China squinted. The white face grew bigger. And still there was no body. China's heart beat fast and hard in her chest.

"Can we go to B.T.'s now?" Deedee asked, her whisper barely audible.

"I want to figure this out," Rick said. "This is incredible."

China couldn't say a word. She couldn't move. She could only watch the face bob and dip and then suddenly disappear and reappear again. Low to the ground, then four feet up, then six, then low again. Nothing she knew could do that. She thought of owls. Owls had wide eyes, but they couldn't move like that. Everything else her mind offered as an explanation, the other part of her mind found a reason to reject.

"Come on, let's go!" Deedee said, her voice in a panic. "Let's get B.T. . . . "

"B.T.!" China shouted. "B.T.! You jerk!" China's mind

suddenly put it all together. The height. The plan. Rick's incredible calm. She slugged Rick. "You're a jerk, too." Then she marched into the forest after the floating face. It disappeared, but China could hear running footsteps. She ran after them. And because she knew the forest a little better than B.T., and because of his hurt toe, she caught him and jumped on his back. Losing his balance, B.T. fell and both of them landed in the dirt.

"You are such a jerk!" China shrieked at him. She grabbed a handful of dirt, yanked off the black cap he wore, and rubbed the dirt in his hair. His black robe fell off and there he was. Regular old B.T. with his ragged jeans, *Family Squabbles* T-shirt, and a very, very white face.

China sat back, shaking her head. She looked from the robe in her hand to the white face. "Rick's right. That was amazing. I've never seen anything like it in my entire life. That beats anything I've ever pulled."

"Were you scared?" B.T. asked, his face eager.

"NO," Deedee said forcefully behind China. "We were not scared. We were curious."

"What a lie," Rick offered. "You were scared out of your minds. I felt your nails digging into my arms; I have the scars to prove it."

"You do not!" Deedee said, delivering a swift side kick to the seat of his pants.

❧

The next morning, the girls walked past the lake on

their way to run an errand for Mr. Kiersey. "What's that?" Deedee pointed out a group of kids on a grassy mound focused on something in front of them.

"It's got to be B.T.," China said, feeling that surge of excitement and pleasure.

"It looks like the Sermon on the Mount," Deedee said. "I wonder if they think he can heal people, too."

China ignored her sarcasm. "I'm going to see what he's up to now. Probably filming more stuff for the banquet."

"Who cares?"

"Excuse me," China said to the kids in front of her, gently pushing them aside. "Excuse me B.T.'s assistant coming through." The kids reluctantly parted. China repeated her message until she'd reached the rock where B.T. sat.

"I didn't know you had an assistant," a tall, skinny kid said to B.T.

"A what?"

The kid pointed at China as she emerged from the crowd. "That chick."

"Hi!" China said enthusiastically. "Here I am! I thought maybe you were filming and you would want me here to help."

"Who do you think you are?" asked the skinny kid. To B.T., he said, "Who does she think she is?"

B.T. shifted on the rock. He put his camera down and looked at her, his eyes cold and hard. "No, thanks. I don't need you, China."

China's heart started beating hard in her chest. "I'm sorry . . . . I just wanted to help."

"I don't need your help, thanks," B.T. said, his voice as cold and hard as his eyes. "I have enough of you on tape. Give someone else a chance."

"But . . . I thought, to be your friend . . . " China wanted to talk to him. To ask him if they were friends. To talk to him about something, anything. She looked up into a dark mass of stares. Her face felt hot. "I'm . . . I'm sorry. I didn't mean to . . . " Confusion made mucky business of her thoughts. She stood and moved forward. The crowd parted again to let her through, this time without her saying anything.

She ran to catch up with Deedee, who hadn't even slowed down to see what B.T. was doing. She walked with her arms swinging fast, her sleeveless blue flannel shirt flapping with the effort. Her hiking boots struck the ground, making dull thuds. "Deedee, wait up."

Deedee walked just as fast, her mahogany curls bouncing with every firm step.

"What is wrong with you?"

"Nothing. I just want to do this errand by myself, okay? Maybe we're spending too much time together."

China stopped and let Deedee go on without her. Instead, she went to Rick's cabin.

"Hi," she said, trying to hide the tears threatening to fall at any wrong word. "Can I take Bologna?"

The little dog raced toward her, his listing tilt pulling him to the right. He jumped all over her, licking her as if she had been missing for three years. "At least you love me, little guy."

"Don't give me that. Name one person who doesn't like you," Rick said.

"Rick," China said in a soft voice, "can I tell you something secret?"

Rick stepped out of the cabin and sat on the stoop. "Sure. I love secrets."

"Have you ever known what God wanted you to do? I mean really known that there was something special he had planned?"

Rick reached over and scratched Bologna on the head. "No," he said sadly. "I've always wished I knew. It seems right to be here at Camp Crazy Bear. But I don't know. I love being silly, singing, and having fun. It seems I can make other people happy with that, too. But I don't see a hot job market for ugly guys who use corny songs to make people smile."

"Isn't there a verse somewhere that says God has a wonderful plan for your life?"

"I'm the wrong person to ask that. I don't know my Bible very well."

China waved her hand in front of her face, hoping the gnats would go find another critter to bother.

"So what's the secret?" Rick asked. "You know what God wants for you?"

China stared through the trees, the side of Magda's cabin visible through the clearing. Bologna licked her nose as she cuddled him up to her face.

"Come on, China. You're not being fair. Now you've got to tell me your secret."

"You promise you won't laugh?"

Rick crossed his heart, sitting perky and silent, a little too eager to listen.

"It's just that I think God's going to use me in a great way." She chewed her lip before she continued. "This is so incredible. If I'm right, I'm going to go somewhere, Rick. I'm going to be somebody. Somebody important. The Heathers of the world will be sorry for everything. The Heathers of the world will wish I were their friend." She got on such a roll, she forgot she was pouring all her secret thoughts out loud. "They'll tell everyone they once knew me, and I'll pretend I didn't know them. I'll do something so great . . . "

"What are you getting at?" Rick asked, his head tilted out and forward as he looked at her almost out of the side of his eyes.

Startled, China realized what she'd done. Clasping her hands together, she smiled and bit her lip. "What if God brought B.T. here so that I could meet him and . . ." Then she couldn't finish.

Rick motioned for her to go on, his face looking almost like it wore the same dark cloud B.T.'s face had.

"Never mind." Maybe it was meant to be private—

too sacred to share.

She jumped up and wiggled her fingers so the deaf dog would follow her. She heard Rick sigh and slap his thigh. She never turned around.

CHAPTER SEVENTEEN

ALL MORNING SHE WANDERED THE TRAILS with Bologna. They sat at the creek, and China threw sticks until it got too hot. She heard the shouts of the kids at the Battlefield playing relays with the atlaspheres. After her little adventure, Kemper decided the level grassy field was a safer place to use them.

The more she was left alone with her thoughts, the bigger they grew. It seemed so clear that God was leading her down the star-studded sidewalks of Hollywood. She tried to picture the inside of a sound stage. She wondered if they filmed outside much. And how they made the inside of the rooms look real. Would she have a dressing room? Did they really have those or was that something someone made up? She wondered if she would get to keep all the clothes they would buy for the shows. Or if she could borrow the cutest ones for special days.

Bologna jumped up and down, trying to get her attention by nipping at her fingers. She picked him up and carried him a little way, and then put him down again.

"Shall we go home and eat lunch now, Bologna?" The little deaf dog wagged his whole behind. He obviously didn't know what she said, but he understood she talked to him. China took off at a slow trot, with Bologna happily dashing ahead after lizards and flying bugs.

China put Bologna on a collar and chain and left him outside the Kiersey cabin. Opening the door, she heard a major commotion going on inside. The little girls were shrieking and running around the room. Eve ran into China, bounced off, and ran in another direction. She could see the corner of Adam's blue shirt as he hid behind the sofa. Then B.T. stomped out of the kitchen as a large, treacherous dinosaur. His hands curled and raised high overhead, his blond hair moussed so it would stick out in dangerous-looking spikes. He had put on something very dark and red all over his mouth. His lips curled, and his teeth were covered with plastic fangs. Snarls gushed out and the girls screamed in terror.

Anna raced over to China. "'Saur!" she screamed, pointing at B.T. She sucked madly on her thumb, her eyes wide with delighted fear. "'Saur!"She ran around and around the room.

"Cover me!" Adam shouted.

Joseph was ready with a Nerf bow and arrow. Adam leapt from his hiding place and tried to knock down the tyrannosaurus rex. But the rex was too mighty, too powerful. Even the flying arrows didn't make him flinch. The rex picked up Adam and plopped him on the ground.

"I'm dying!" screamed Adam. "I'm dying a horrible, terrible, bloody death."

With a roaring snarl, the rex moved into Adam's neck for the kill. Adam obliged by writhing dramatically for a bit, then lying still.

"What are you doing here?" China asked.

"Deedee invited me to lunch. She said I needed to see how the other 90 percent lives."

Joseph grabbed his arm and tried to twist it behind his back. B.T. whipped him around and had him flat on his back in no time. B.T. pretended nothing had happened.

"Where's Deedee?"

B.T. shrugged. "I think she's in her room or something."

China marched back to where Deedee read a book on mountain survival. "I don't get it."

"Huh?" Deedee looked up from her book.

"I thought you didn't like B.T. I thought you said he was a fake."

"I figured I should give him another chance. And I thought the kids would have fun with him here. And they are. Is there anything wrong with that?"

Of course there was nothing wrong with that. But China's future loomed large and exclusive. "Are you trying to butt in? Did you want to get alone with B.T. so you could steal my rightful place? I can't believe you'd invite him and not tell me."

Deedee sailed the book across the room. "You weren't around for me to tell. I had no idea where you were this morning. I thought of it as I passed by the Battlefield. B.T. had just come out of an atlasphere. I had to find out what he thought of it."

China felt like she'd been running. Her breath came in short, quick puffs. Nothing seemed clearly defined. Her thoughts and beliefs blurred. *Am I right or not?*

"I don't want to steal your stupid friend. If you want to make a fool out of yourself, then go right ahead. Just leave me out of it."

China didn't know what to do. She didn't like the anger parading in twitches all over Deedee's face. She knew her own signs of exploding anger rumbling beneath the surface. It happened too many times with her family for her not to recognize what was about to happen. Words would fall out of her mouth she would later regret. But right now she didn't care. She threw her words as pointed nails, aiming for Deedee's soft spots.

"Fine. You'll be sorry someday when you see who I really am. You'll be sorry."

"Who are you really?" Deedee asked her. "I thought I knew."

"Somebody special. Somebody important."

"My, girl! That's some attitude you're carrying. You

sure you're not on drugs?"

"Funny!"

"Well, if you're serious, and you're not on drugs, you can just find yourself a new friend. Because I'm not having anything to do with you."

"Okay. I was going to take you to Greece. Or Madagascar. Or somewhere fun. I thought we'd have a great time traveling together."

Deedee looked like she'd swallowed an egg whole and it got jammed somewhere halfway down. She was quiet, almost not breathing, her face stuck in that gawking position. Then the air came out. "I've changed my mind. I don't want to go to Greece."

"Okay. Where do you want to go?"

"You don't get it, do you?"

B.T. knocked on the doorjamb. "Hey, Deedee. The natives are getting a little too restless. And they've worn me out. Can I help you get lunch or anything?"

"Tell him, China. Tell him what you think."

B.T. looked from one angry face to the other. "Ooops! I'll go back to the natives. It'll probably be safer there."

"No, B.T.," Deedee said, smiling with sarcasm. "Please ask China what's been going on in her head these days. Why she's getting to be stuck up. Why she thinks she's better than Heather."

"I'm not anything like Heather," China protested.

"Who's Heather?" B.T. asked.

Deedee got off her bed, arms crossed stiffly in front

of her. "A stuck-up snob who thinks the world is supposed to revolve around her. China had a run-in with her the first week of camp. I thought China was different from Heather. I guess I was wrong." Deedee pushed past B.T., shoving him into the hallway.

China's anger left the room with Deedee. She sighed. "I can't tell whether she just doesn't understand or if she's jealous."

B.T. looked at her, waiting for her to continue.

"I probably shouldn't have told her. I should have kept it to myself. But I was so excited. God made it so clear. Clearer than anything I've ever experienced." China looked down the hall at Deedee trying to settle down her brothers and sisters. "Come on in here and sit down. I guess it's about time I tell you."

B.T. shook his head. "We can go outside. I don't think it's right for us to be in a room alone . . . "

"Oh, yeah. Sorry. I wasn't thinking."

The two went out front and sat on the porch steps. China let Bologna off his chain so he could play fetch while she and B.T. talked.

"After we went to dinner the other night, I was sitting by the lake. And the more I thought about what you said about making a decision about your world, the more I knew the answer. I realized why all this happened."

"All what?"

"Me coming to camp, meeting Deedee, and all that."

"So why did it happen?"

"So I could meet you."

B.T. smiled. "That's nice, but I doubt God brought you all the way from Guatemala just to meet me."

"It wasn't just to meet you. It was so you could meet me. So God could take me in the direction he really wanted me to go."

"And that is?"

"Into movies. Television. I think God has a ministry for me there. And here you are to make that happen. We got to know each other fast. I bet God did that so you would feel comfortable about asking me to be on your show. And then you can help me get an agent. And then, as they say, 'the rest will be history.'"

China smiled at him, proud, relieved she had finally told him. Her smile faded fast when she saw B.T.'s face. His whole body. Somehow they took out all that stuff that made him alive. He slumped over, his hair covering most of both eyes. "How could you think that, China? Did I ever make you think that? Did I do something to tell you I would help you? Did going out to dinner do this to you?" B.T. slammed his fist on the steps. "I knew it was going to backfire on me. It was the totally wrong thing to do."

"No! It wasn't the wrong thing to do. That's what opened my ears to God's voice. I know God talked to me through that."

"Maybe it wasn't God, China."

China's eyes narrowed. "How do you know it wasn't

God? You don't know."

"It doesn't work that way, China. You live in the wrong place. You have the wrong look. You don't even have any acting talent."

"How do you know I don't have any acting talent?"

"I filmed you, remember?"

"I wasn't really trying."

"It doesn't matter. There's something missing."

"I'm funny. I make people laugh."

"In a different way. You are a wonderful person. But . . . " B.T. stopped. "You're right. I don't know if God spoke to you or not. But he didn't tell me that. I thought we were going to be good friends. The three of us."

Friends?

B.T. stood up and shoved his hands in his pockets. "Tell Deedee I'm sorry I couldn't stay for lunch. It was nice knowing you, China."

"What do you mean?"

"I mean I can't be friends with you. I can't lead you on like this. I can't let you think I'm the answer to all your dreams. If God wants you on TV, he's going to have to do it some other way. He's going to have to make it happen. I can't do it. I'm tired of people using me to get into the biz. I won't do it anymore." His voice sounded wounded. "I really thought you were different." He walked down the steps and started down the trail.

China looked after him. For a brief moment, it occurred to China that she had ruined it all. But then another thought blasted in and took over. *God, you're just going to have to show him I'm right. You'll have to show him this is all part of your plan.*

As China hooked Bologna back up to the chain, it was as if some tiny insect were trying to gnaw away at the inside of her. As if it tried to get her attention or tell her something. She crushed it and threw it away before it could do any damage.

CHAPTER EIGHTEEN

ALL AFTERNOON CHINA MOVED ABOUT THE kitchen in a grumble. Nothing went right. She didn't want to do anything Magda asked her to do. All she could see was how Magda talked an awful lot like a backwoods hick. And how Rick acted so stupid. How they both were going nowhere in life. They would spend their lives in nowhere being nobodies. She was thrilled when her shift ended and she could get out.

China slipped into the back of Sweet Pea Lodge, anxious to see Kemper's new plan at work. Instead of doing something silly and gross, he planned something serious and gross. As soon as China heard he had planned a massive foot washing, she was sure it wouldn't work. Not with a bunch of kids. Not with a bunch of smelly feet. No one would do it. But if they did, she wanted to see it.

Kemper had dimmed the lights. Probably so no one would be embarrassed. Maybe so he wouldn't be embarrassed if no one moved from their seat. He had placed the chairs in little half-moon circles around the room. A stack of towels and small soap chips lay next to buckets. One bucket for every half moon. One soap chip and towel for every person.

The kids sat awkwardly in their seats. Lots of them shifted about, some whispered, but most were uncharacteristically silent. Kemper quietly explained what he expected them to do. China waited to see if anyone would really do it. Sure, Jesus had washed the feet of his disciples. But that was different. He was God. A thought crossed her mind. *If he was God, then* they *should have been washing* his *feet.* She didn't like the doors opening inside her head. She didn't like the feeling that something was trying to get her attention. So she shut it off and paid attention to the show she'd come to watch.

Taped worship music played in the background almost so low she couldn't hear it. But no one moved. Kemper looked out among the crowd. China could see on his face that he wanted to talk. His black mustache twitched over his lip. He pulled the pencil from the patch of wiry hair he kept for just that purpose. He stabbed it back in again. "You may begin now," he said for the second time.

Off to one side, China saw someone get up, get a bucket, and go outside. When he returned, she saw it was B.T. All eyes were on him. Some girls sat up straighter. You could tell they were hopeful. Like in elementary school when being the best kid in class meant the teacher would pick you to do some marvelous chore like take a note to the office or erase the board. B.T. was like the teacher, with all power to bless someone with his presence. Oh, how China longed to be in his shoes! To be wanted like that. To be admired. *Well, it's not too long from now that I'll be there*, she thought.

China figured B.T. would go to the cutest girl there— Bonnie. But he didn't. He kept walking. He stopped in front of . . .

No. He wouldn't. He couldn't.

B.T. knelt on the floor and began untying the beat-up tennis shoes of Kevin. Kevin was not only the ugliest kid China had ever seen, he was probably one of the fattest. Kids had avoided him all week. The guys in his cabin made sure everyone knew Kevin had not taken one shower that week. Or brushed his teeth. China was sure the rumors were true. She could smell Kevin long before she could see him. And right now he was sitting alone. The halfmoon had turned into a straight line of three chairs as kids had dismantled it so they wouldn't have to sit next to him.

And there was B.T., peeling off socks that had probably been white sometime in the prehistoric past. Instead, they were some sort of dingy brown or gray. B.T. didn't back off or flinch. He plunked Kevin's left foot into the water and began washing.

Murmurs traveled through the room. Then kids all over the room began getting up, taking buckets, and carrying them outside to fill.

China didn't know what to make of it. B.T. washing someone's feet? Especially someone like Kevin? Why? He didn't have to. He was the superstar. He was the one everyone would die a thousand deaths if they could wash his feet. He could have washed anyone's feet. But he chose the ugliest kid that no one liked.

See? words said inside her. *B.T. doesn't see himself as better than others. He gives of himself in little ways. He sees that others really enjoy his company . . . and he's friendly to them. He gets tired of phoniness, but he's still trying to serve.*

China sighed. She liked the glory in being recognized. B.T. had both, and so could she.

She was so focused on this totally amazing thing going on that she didn't hear someone come up to her.

"You're part of the kitchen staff, aren't you?" A guy stood in front of her. He was holding a bucket and a towel was draped over his arm.

China felt like Peter. She wanted to deny it. She wanted to say, "No, I'm not. I never knew anyone on the kitchen staff. You think I'd even associate with them? I'm going to be in Hollywood soon. I have a far more important job than working in a kitchen." That's what she wanted to say. But maybe she could say that next summer. The kid stood there with big eyes and a bucket of water, waiting for her answer. China opened her mouth to deny it. But she had to be honest. "Yeah," she told the kid, her eyes turned away, embarrassed at the lowly place she held.

"Then may I wash your feet?"

China turned her head so fast, hair got stuck in her mouth. "Why?"

The kid didn't look like he was making fun of her. He looked totally serious. "I know you worked hard this week. I watched you. And at the beginning you really were happy. It was like you really enjoyed serving us. And when I had KP, I saw you always doing stuff and not complaining when it wasn't really stuff most kids would do. Anyway, I wanted to be the one to wash your feet. Kind of like a thank-you. My mom cleans at the church and no one ever thanks her. Maybe I'm doing this as a thank-you to her, too."

"Uh," China said awkwardly, shame melting her heart into a puddle of tears. "You don't have to. I only came in to watch. I've never seen something like this before."

The boy's steady gaze held hers. "I want to. It would be a privilege."

The boy untied her shoes and gently took them off. He peeled off her socks next. China thought she'd die of embarrassment. But the kid didn't seem to care that she had dirty brown lines around the ankles. He didn't seem to care that her feet were a little moist from the heat. He took each one in turn, dipped it in the water, washed it thoroughly with soap, then dried it with a towel. As he went about his task, he thanked her for specific things he'd seen her do.

China tried to hold back her tears. She held her breath, bit her lip, dug her nails into her hands. And then the silent sobs came, followed by sniffles. And heavy breathing. His tender touch. His unbelievable willingness to serve her. To thank her.

When the guy finished, China thanked him. The tears poured down her face. But nothing in his face made her feel ashamed of her tears. He said, "Thank you," and walked away.

China watched him go, her heart so full of shame. So amazed at what she'd spent her days thinking about. How important she was. How important she could be.

B.T. appeared on stage, guitar in hand. In a quiet voice, so as not to disturb those still washing, he sang a song about service. He sang the words Jesus had told his disciples about how important it is to serve others. And how the ones who serve were really important, not those who were served. And not those that seemed to be the most important.

China slipped out the back, her freshly washed feet reminding her with every step that she had been running in the wrong direction. She had let lies and a crazy imagination twist everything she had ever known and believed. She started to trot, then run as fast as she could to Eelapuash. She pushed open the door, glad someone was still there. She hoped it was Magda.

"My, my, China honey," Magda said, sweater draped over her arm. "I was just gonna get to my cabin. What's goin' on inside your head?"

"Magda, I'm so sorry!"

"What for?"

"Can you just come sit down for a minute?"

"Sure, China honey."

China led her into the dining hall and had her sit in a chair turned away from the table. "I'll be right back."

She ran into the kitchen and found a large mixing bowl. She partially filled it with warm water, grabbed the liquid soap and a dish towel. Back in the dining hall, she knelt in front of Magda and began to take off her shoes and socks. Her lumpy feet were hot and sweaty. They were discolored from many years and many hours of standing on them, with many pounds to support. She began to wash the lumpy feet.

"Magda, I've never thanked you enough. I've never understood why you would be satisfied with such a thankless job. Now I understand. You are serving God and loving every minute of it. I want you to know how much I appreciate you. It's my privilege to serve you.

"You are always willing to listen. You are never too busy. I bet you are the most important person at Camp Crazy Bear." The light came on in China's heart, chasing all the darkness away. She rocked back on her haunches as the truth hit her full force.

"Why, Magda—without you, or someone like you,

there could not be a high school camp!"

Magda looked down and actually blushed.

And for the second time that night, China cried.

CHAPTER NINETEEN

As China towel-dried Magda's feet, the door to the dining hall opened. China turned to see B.T. standing in the doorway. She dropped her head and turned back to Magda.

"I'm sorry," B.T. whispered. "I didn't mean to interrupt." The door swung shut, and Magda and China were alone once more.

China replaced Magda's socks and food-spotted comfortable nursing shoes. It wasn't until she stood and hugged Magda that she realized Magda was crying. "Lan' sakes, child," Magda said, her voice barely over a whisper. "You do know how to make a woman cry."

They stood, locked in a hug, tears drenching the shoulders of the other, for a long time. China moved back so she could look into Magda's fading brown eyes.

"I've never met anyone who serves with as much joy as you do. I bet Jesus is awfully proud to have a kid like you around, Magda."

Magda started to chuckle through her tears. "Me a 'kid.' I guess you're right. I ain't nothin' but God's child.

176

And nothin' could be better than that."

Silently they walked through the dining hall and kitchen, shutting out lights. Then, arm in arm, they walked up the path to Magda's house, where China gave her another hug and a kiss on the cheek good night.

The mountain didn't seem frightening or lonely. Every pine-scented breath China took seemed to clear out the cobwebs that had been taking over her mind. The stars were pinpoints of light in a dark night. Like the things she was learning. Pinpoints of truth in a dark world. She walked slowly, not wanting the night to end. Not wanting to miss walking with God anymore. She knew he was right there. People would think she was nuts if she tried to describe it to them. But it was true. He was as real as if she could see him walking there. As real as if his feet put footprints next to hers. She could swear dust was billowing up around feet she couldn't see.

God, I can't believe what an idiot I've been, she prayed. *Here I've been calling B.T. a jerk when I'm the jerk.*

The tears started again. Not heavy. Just little ones. Like a gentle rain shower cleansing the air.

How dare I think God has a plan to make me better than everyone else! For the second time that day, the feeling of lightning shot through China. *God doesn't want to make me better than everyone else. He wants to make me a servant to everyone else. I don't have to wish God would make me special. I already am.*

Little Bear Lake beckoned to her. She sat on the shore

and watched its surface ruffle in the breeze. She hugged her knees to her chest and sat without thinking much. Just resting in the knowledge that who she was and how she served was more important than money or fame or all the goodies life could give her. She sighed. *They sure would be nice, though, God. If you ever decide to give them to me, I sure won't turn them down.* She smiled.

"Can I sit here?"

She looked up into B.T.'s solemn face. His hair, always, always hovering over his right eye.

"I guess. If you can stand to be with me." Inside her stirred something odd. It wasn't the crazy, compelling mystery that had made her crazy about B.T. It was different. He had a heart that really was different from most guys China had known. It was who he was on the inside that made her desperately want to be his friend. Good friends. It didn't matter that he was male. It didn't matter that he was famous. Or rich. She actually wished he wasn't those things. It would make things far less complicated.

B.T. dropped onto the sand next to her. "I'm sorry," he started. He drew something in the sand with his finger. It was too dark for China to see what it was. "I really was a jerk. I put you into the category of all the wanna-bes I see all the time. I was wrong. You're really special, China."

China put her forehead on her knees. Her heart beat faster. She knew that meant she was about to tell him the truth about herself. The truth she didn't like to admit. But if she was going to be friends with him, she had to let him know. Then he could decide whether or not to still be friends with her.

"No, B.T. You were right. Please. Let me be the jerk here. Somehow I figured I needed to be a Hollywood-type person to really be your friend. And so I started thinking too hard."

"But you are my friend, China."

China shook her head. "You could never really be my friend."

B.T.'s face fell, and he went back to drawing in the sand.

"I could never be pretty enough, rich enough, stylish enough, or act right enough to be your friend."

"Don't you get it, China? That's exactly what I don't want in a friend. I want someone who's funny and loves God and other people and knows what it means to be a Christian in real life, not just in words. I don't care what the outside package is. There are a lot of Barbie dolls out there. They tend to be so pretty on the outside, it doesn't matter what they are like inside. What I want in a friend is right here in front of me."

China chewed on her cheek. It was too hard to believe that B.T. could really want her as a friend. "But I've been such a jerk."

She waited for B.T. to say something. But he kept silent. China took B.T.'s silence to mean she should keep talking. The covering of darkness helped her to say things she would be too shy to say again.

"I don't know why I wanted so badly to be your

friend. I felt some kind of crazy connection with you. And after our dinner I thought your wanting to show us your way of living was also your invitation to step inside your world. That thought led me to think about that idea until I stupidly thought maybe God brought you here so I could be on television. Witness to the masses. Get rich. Buy my camp. I got so involved in the dream, I forgot what's really most important."

"You know, Chi . . . it isn't as glamorous as people make it seem."

"You said that before. But I guess I didn't believe you."

"Sometimes it's fun. But it really gets old after a while. I make fun so I can survive it."

"So why do you stay?"

"Because parts of it are fun. And because I think God opened doors for me for some reason I don't know yet. It's hard for me to not get caught up in it all. It looks so great on the outside. Kind of like a Lotus. Or Lamborghini. Or a Lear jet. Smooth. Fast. Cool. But on the inside, it can be pretty rotten. There's some awful people in this business. They don't care who they hurt or what they produce, just so long as they make big money fast."

B.T. kept drawing in the sand. China watched the ripples on the lake. Little dark peaks and darker valleys.

"I envy you here, China. Being able to serve. To give and give and give."

"WHAT? You envy me? I envy you!"

B.T. laughed. "You know what they always say . . . "

"The grass is always greener . . . " they said in unison.

B.T. put his head back and laughed. "You know, China, I think you're very wrong."

China's heart stopped. "About what?"

"I believe that you and I can be real good friends."

China turned her head slowly, afraid if she turned too fast the moment would disappear into thin air. "You do? Even after I've been such a jerk?"

"You've seen the error of your ways and left them behind. I'm sure of that. Part of a great friendship is being honest and forgiving each other." Even in the darkness, China could see B.T. winked.

"I sure hope so."

"I think we understand each other more than you think."

China searched his face. She could see he wasn't playing a game or trying to make her feel good. He was telling the truth. Everything she saw in his eyes showed there was an open door to friendship. She decided to open her heart in return. "I've always thought we could be friends. From the moment you pulled me up behind you on that horse, I knew. But I really didn't think you felt the same."

"I knew the moment I saw the daggers coming out of your eyes when you were stuck in that atlasphere. But I wasn't sure. I'd never met anyone I connected with like that. It was like we'd always known each other. Always been friends."

"Yeah."

"But I was scared."

"Me, too."

B.T. put his hand out as if to shake hers. China wiped her sandy hand on her side and put her hand in his. "Friends?" he asked.

"Friends," she answered.

B.T. stood, lifting her to her feet. "Friends don't shake hands. They give hugs."

China got lost in one of the sweetest hugs she'd ever experienced.

"You know," B.T. said, a smile in his voice, "I think I've just found my million-dollar friend."

⤸

"Where were you?" Deedee asked, yawning. "I was about to send out a search party."

"I went to the meeting, and then I . . . well, I wanted to sit by the lake and think."

"Mmmm."

"Deeds?"

"Yeah?"

"I've been an absolute, total, 100-percent jerk. I'm sorry. I hope you can forgive me for yelling at you. For becoming a first-class snot and an idiot. I wouldn't blame you if you hated me forever." China paused and sighed heavily. She still couldn't look Deedee in the eye. "You were right. My dream was so incredibly stupid. Next time I'll try to listen to you."

Deedee was quiet a moment. "Okay. Are you sure you don't want to be on TV?"

China blew a raspberry. "Why would I want to be on TV when I can face bears, atlaspheres, Heathers, food poisoning, and other dangers on a daily basis with my best friend?"

Deedee jumped up from her bed, heaved her pillow at China, then dove after it. She gave her a quick hug, snagged her pillow, and dove back into bed again.

~∂

The next morning Kemper had planned an open lake day. The slide, Blob, and diving dock were getting heavy use. China helped Deedee with the boats as kids loaded them to the limit and paddled about the lake. "Look!" Deedee pointed. "Isn't that B.T. about to go off the Blob? What about his stitches?"

"Last night he said he was not going to leave camp until he went off the Blob. He said he wouldn't miss such an adrenaline rush for anything."

The girls watched B.T. climb the ladder. At the top, he listened to the instructions from the lifeguard, nodded, then held on to the railings. He rocked back and forth, ready to run down the ramp and jump.

"I have a bad feeling about this," China breathed.

At that moment, B.T. took off running. In three steps, he was off the tower, falling toward the Blob. As he landed, the boy at the other end catapulted toward the sky, a WHOOP! filling the air. At the same instant the boy hit the water, Deedee put her hands on the counter and said, "Where's B.T.?"

China looked at the Blob. It didn't look right. It was still big and pillowy. But B.T. wasn't there. "Maybe he slid off the other side."

"I didn't see him."

The lifeguards sprang into action, five of them swimming frantically toward the Blob.

"Something's happening," Deedee said. "They don't send that many lifeguards for nothing."

China slammed the cash box into a trunk, locked it, and both girls took off running. On the shore, China pulled off her T-shirt and dove into the water. She'd never been a great swimmer, but she focused on making the most powerful strokes she could muster.

When she got to the Blob, she could hear an odd sound coming from somewhere inside.

"Well, he's laughing," Eagle, the head lifeguard, mentioned.

"Where is he?" China asked, treading water.

"The seam to the outer cover ripped," explained Shark.

"Split right between the red and the blue stripe," Eagle said, shaking his head. "Just enough for him to slip inside."

"How could that happen?" asked Shark. "I've never heard of it happening before. Has it?"

"Not to my knowledge."

"It will probably never happen again," China said, laughing.

The lifeguards turned to look at her.

"It's B.T. This kind of stuff happens to him."

"How do we get him out?" Water Lily asked.

Eagle swam around the Blob. "We'll have to cut him out. There's no way he can climb back up on the bladder. And there's no other way around it."

"Serdab!" called B.T. "Trilobite!"

"I can't believe you, B.T.!" China called. "You are too crazy."

"It's my rescuer! My lady in shining swimsuit come to my rescue once again!" came B.T.'s voice from inside the cloth.

"Dream on, buddy! I'm letting someone else rescue you this time. This one's out of my league. I'm going to the shore where it's safe."

"Some friend you are!" he called.

"Deal with it, big boy." China swam back to shore. She and Deedee sat on the sand sipping root beer and eating a bag of Chee-Tos cheese puffs while they waited for their crazy friend to reappear. "I think I'm going to miss him a bunch," China told her.

"My dad's not going to miss him," Deedee said. "He's going to breathe a sigh of relief."

Cheers erupted all around when the Blob gave birth to a strapping boy. Deedee put her fingers to her lips and whistled. China stuck a Chee-To in her mouth and clapped loudly.

B.T. swam to the shore. As he stepped from the

water, he gave a bow. Everyone cheered and applauded again. Walking toward the girls, he said, "Well, now that's over, nothing else can happen today."

China opened her mouth and pointed at the sand. But it was too late. B.T.'s foot met the wasp and invented a new dance step.

"It's not funny!" B.T. yelled, his face red with pain. His words didn't even make a slight dent in China's, and Deedee's hysterical laughter.

Don't Miss China's First Three Unforgettable Adventures!

There's more action and excitement as China adjusts to life at Camp Crazy Bear. Although she's enjoying her independence, China finds that getting herself into trouble is easier than learning the biblical truths God wants to teach her.

Sliced Heather on Toast
Heather Hamilton, the snobby camp queen, has it in for China from the moment they meet. It soon turns into a week-long war of practical jokes, hurt feelings, and valuable lessons.

The Secret Kitchen
After becoming an employee of Camp Crazy Bear, China and her friend Deedee adopt a deaf, stray dog . . . even though it's against camp rules. Meanwhile, someone's planning a devious scheme that could cause great danger to China!

Project Black Bear
Thinking it would be fun to have live bears for pets, China and Deedee set out food in an effort to lure the animals into camp. But these are wild California black bears, and the girls' good intentions have disastrous results.

Available at your favorite Christian bookstore.

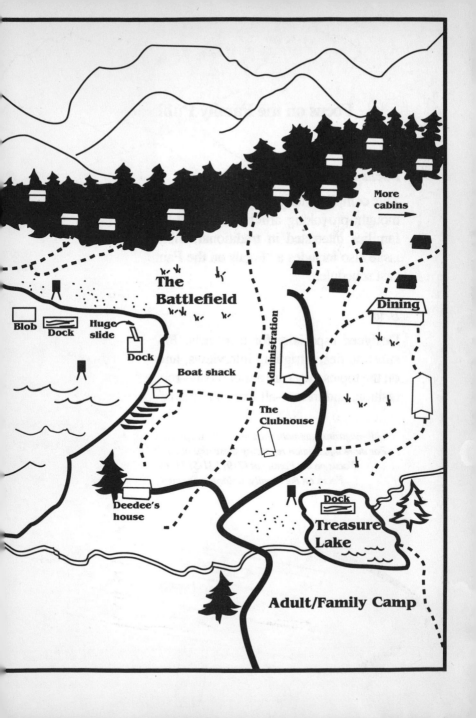

More cabins →

The
Battlefield

Dining

Administration

Blob

Dock

Huge
slide

Dock

Boat shack

The Clubhouse

Deedee's
house

Dock

Treasure
Lake

Adult/Family Camp

ications

inspiring stories,
l information for
cal values. Each
ily" radio broad-

o is packed with
l amusing articles
ationships, fitness,
n perspective.

ere otherwise noted.
resources, please call
r write to us at
, CO 80995